The Jackson Children
and the
DRAGON
HUNT

Book one of the Jackson Chronicles

Published by PJK Publishing

Printed in the United Kingdom

The Jackson Children
and the
DRAGON HUNT

Book one of the Jackson Chronicles

MacKenzie Keeble

Although specifically written for children of 8 to 15 years of age, it is an exciting adventure story that can be read by, or to, all children. However, this story can also be enjoyed by the older members of the family. It is imaginative and fantastic, featuring magical creatures, but is written in a way that makes it believable and includes life lessons for the youngsters. What we used to call 'a moral to the story'. The monsters are friendly, it's easy to read and a lot of fun.

READERS COMMENTS:

This wonderful story takes you on a mythical, exciting journey. The curiosity of the three children leads to mesmerizing adventures. My family can't wait for the next one!

– Dannii Lindsay (author)

I wanted to read this book for two reasons. Firstly, due to my family name and secondly, to check its suitability for my grandchildren. I was very pleasantly surprised. I found it very entertaining and fun to read. It is an exciting book and will inspire imaginative young minds to read.

– Les Jackson

My 14-year-old enjoyed it so much, I started reading it to my 8-year-old and couldn't put it down.

– Rachel

I read it to my child and enjoyed it as much as she did.

– Brendan

When I couldn't give my daughter the next book in the series, Julia cried. I don't remember her enjoying a book so much.

– Reginald T.

In memory of my father,
Henry John Keeble,
who loved to tell a story.
He passed away on
7th June 2010
and is always on my mind.

Acknowledgements

Without the love, support and encouragement of my family, Sandra my understanding and patient wife, Joshua and Matthew my wonderful sons, who were being continually told to be quiet as 'Daddy is writing', this book would never have been possible.

I wish to also sincerely thank my sons Joshua and Matthew for their teenage critique, feedback, comments and guidance, in respect of this story.

I also wish to acknowledge and thank Spiffing Covers. Their staff have been inspirational and their guidance has been invaluable in the creation of this series.

Talking about writing, Ernest Hemingway is quoted as saying: 'We are all apprentices in a craft where no one ever becomes a master.'

Whereas Gene Fowler is quoted as saying: 'Writing is easy. All you do is stare at a blank sheet of paper until drops of blood form on your head.'

Leo Tolstoy however is quoted as saying: 'One ought only to write when one leaves a piece of one's own flesh in the inkpot, each time one dips one's pen.'

I can honestly say that despite the fact that I put my heart and soul into the writing of this book, my forehead did not bleed and neither did I leave pieces of my flesh in the inkwell. However, I would love to think that my hard work was worthwhile and the reader enjoyed my story, which at the end of the day is my true wish.

ILLUSTRATIONS

The front and rear covers, plus the spine of the book are the creative work of Spiffing Covers, who have passed the copyright to the author.

The illustrations in the book, unless mentioned below, have been drawn by Amy Rushton. The author wishes to thank Amy for her insight and talent in creating the images she has portrayed for the story, and also to thank her for passing copyright of these images to the author.

The images of the dragons and the eggs were drawn by Simon Rushton, who has kindly passed copyright to the author.

The images of the goblins, the mountain troll, the cottage and the map at the beginning of the book are drawn by the author.

ILLUSTRATIONS

The Jackson Family iii

The Journey from the Cottage to the Cave 2

A Windy Night 6

Jenny, the mother 8

Adam loves cookies 11

The Moving Van 16

Minafon Cottage 18

Ground Floor plan of Cottage 23

Upstairs plan of Cottage 23

Jenny climbing up to the Loft 31

Jenny in the Loft 35

The Children start to explore the Loft 44

Katie, the older sister 51

The Children find the first Clue 59

The Village Sign 66

Jacqui, the younger sister 71

They meet Noogan 80

The Children come out of the Wood 84

The Stone Bridge 90

The old lady's feet didn't seem
to quite reach the ground 95

The Clue they found on the bridge 99

Sparkie, making herself at home
on Jacqui's bed 109

Adam, the youngest 117

Gothic, a huge Mountain Troll 122

Joker, a serious Goblin 127

Sofire, awakes to greet the children 133

Sofire raises her head and calls Tinsel 139

Tinsel, The Elven Queen 142

Sofire reveals the eggs 146

The Precious Dragon Egg 163

CONTENTS

Chapter 1: The Scary Noises 5

Chapter 2: The Day Before: The Move 16

Chapter 3: The Loft 28

Chapter 4: The Humming Noise Returns 36

Chapter 5: The Search for the Treasure Chest ... 43

Chapter 6: The Discovery 52

Chapter 7: The First Clue 60

Chapter 8: Follow the River 68

Chapter 9: They Meet 'Noogan' 75

Chapter 10: Magic, Scary or Just Weird? 86

Chapter 11: The Adventure Continues 96

Chapter 12: 'Sparkie' 106

Chapter 13: Journey to the Cave 112

Chapter 14: Life or Death? 120

Chapter 15: 'Sofire' 132

Chapter 16: The Elven Queen 140

Chapter 17: The Dream Becomes Reality 150

Chapter 18: The Magical World 157

        The Epilogue 161

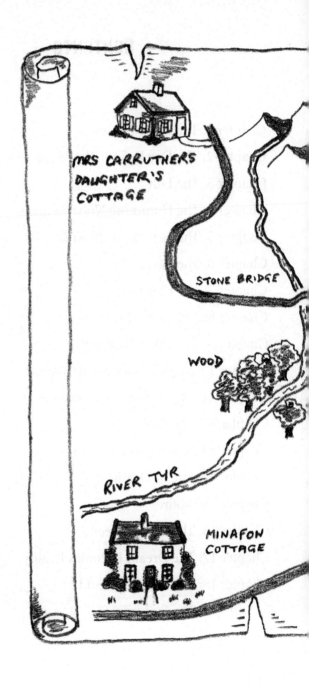

WELSH MOUNTAINS

VILLAGE
SHOP

ROAD TO CWMTYR

Chapter 1
THE SCARY NOISES

Jenny lay on her back in bed in the dark, unable to sleep, too many thoughts and worries in her head. Her three children, however, were so tired after moving house, that they had fallen asleep very quickly. Jenny hadn't told the children that the old lady, who'd previously lived there, had died in the house, or about the rumours that she had been a witch. Children's imagination can run riot, even for her eldest, Katie, who was 15 years of age. The kids had gone through enough over the last two years, with their father's death and all the resulting financial problems.

At least Jenny didn't have to worry about the children starting at their new school yet. The new term didn't start until the first week of September, in six weeks' time. However, Jenny did have a new job at a care home and was starting there on Monday, in two days' time, and that meant 12-hour shifts. Twelve hours at a time, away from the children. For the last two years, apart from when they were at school, Jenny hadn't left the children for two minutes, let alone 12 hours! Whilst at work Jenny would be continuously worrying about the children being sensible and staying safe.

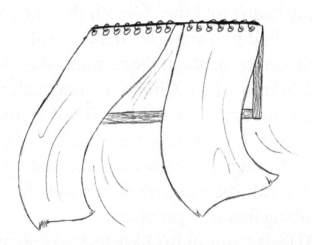

'A windy night'

Right now though, she needed sleep, but sleep seemed a long way away. Outside it was blowing a gale and the wind was whistling through the gaps in the old window frames. There was a scary howling down the chimney and every part of the 200-year-old cottage seemed to be groaning.

Even the stairs were creaking, which in an unfamiliar house in the dark, made it sound as though someone kept walking up and down the stairs. The children would be very scared if they knew about the stories of the witch and the death in the house. With her husband, Jack, having only died two years ago, she knew she mustn't let her imagination run away either. Jenny knew all these sounds would also be there in the daytime, but at night, in the dark, the sounds were all magnified and seemed to become sinister. She lay there in the dark listening to the sounds, trying to adjust to them, trying to accept them.

Then she began to notice a low, gentle humming noise that appeared to come from immediately above her head. She

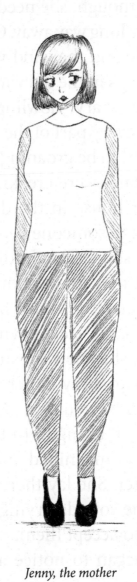

Jenny, the mother

assumed it would be from the loft. The gas boiler would be off now and, at any rate, the boiler was located in the kitchen, not in the loft.

What would be located in the loft that would be making a humming noise? she thought. She lay there trying to work it out. She missed her husband, Jack, all the time, but at times like this she was desperate for a cuddle and his reassuring voice. She certainly wasn't going up there in the loft alone, at night, in the dark. That would have to wait until tomorrow. She was, however, very tired after the move and eventually fell asleep wondering what the humming noise was.

When she woke up in the morning, everything seemed quiet and she jumped out of bed, washed and dressed, and then went around the cottage opening all the curtains and a few of the windows as well, to get some light and fresh air inside. The cottage had been closed up tight since the old lady died over a year ago. The cottage immediately seemed less scary and she started making breakfast for them all.

"Katie! Jacqui! Adam! Breakfast! Up you get," she shouted up the stairs. Even with the curtains pulled back and a few windows open, the inside of the cottage was still gloomy, with brown woodwork and carpets, dark wallpaper and heavy curtains. The cottage cried out for cream walls, white woodwork and nice, new bright curtains. Right now though, Jenny could hardly afford any food, so that would all have to wait.

After they had had breakfast they all climbed in their car and went to search for a local 'corner' shop. They found one near the village and as they walked in they were greeted with, "Bore da!", which means good morning in Welsh.

Jenny cheerfully replied, "Bore da," but quickly explained and apologised to the shop owner that she didn't actually speak Welsh, so the shop owner didn't continue in Welsh. They bought some sausages, four tins of baked beans, cheese,

'Adam loves cookies'

eggs, bread, milk and a torch with two batteries. Jenny put the batteries in the torch to check they were the correct ones for the torch and also to check the torch worked. It worked fine. Then as she was taking six 100-watt light bulbs off a shelf, she noticed Adam had spotted a large jar of 'Fresh home-cooked Welsh recipe biscuits'. Without asking he had taken the jar off the sales counter.

Jenny immediately told Adam to put it back and then said to the shopkeeper, "I am really sorry, but my son loves 'cookies'. How much are they?" The shopkeeper said she made them herself and sold them individually, so Jenny bought four.

As they left the shop Katie said, "Mum, do you know any other Welsh words?"

"Not many lovey, in fact only three. 'Bore da' means good day or good morning. 'Nos da' means goodnight and 'Diolch' means thank you. You can travel around the whole of Wales with those three phrases. Just by saying good morning, goodnight and thank you in their language, you are showing respect to the Welsh people and their culture. However, as we are now going to be living here, we need to start learning the language. You will probably get Welsh language lessons at your new school," Jenny replied.

"Oh, I'll do my best Mum."

"I know you will Katie. The three of you have been wonderful, supporting me through the last two years." And with that Jenny leant forward and kissed Katie on the cheek. They put the goods in the boot of the car and started to drive back, but then Jenny noticed that the gauge showed they were running low on fuel. Not surprising after the long drive up from Hastings. She drove around the village until she spotted a garage and put £10 of petrol in the tank. Jenny couldn't afford any more and, at any rate, she didn't think she would need much petrol in future. Both the village and her new job where only about a mile from the cottage.

When they got back to the cottage they unloaded their shopping and Jenny then changed the light bulbs in the hall, lounge, dining room, kitchen and bathroom, for the new 100-watt bulbs, which left one new bulb as a spare.

She put that with the old weak bulbs, in a kitchen cupboard, for emergency backup. Then she made tea for everyone and they tried the local recipe Welsh biscuits. They were really good.

After tea, Jenny couldn't put it off any longer. She had to know what was making that noise in the loft, but she certainly wasn't going to say that to the children. She just explained to them she wanted to find out if the loft was boarded, that is, could they walk around in the loft? Also, had the previous owner left any junk up there?

"Listen guys, this will be fun," Jenny said. "This is a very old cottage and the old lady may have left anything up there. Sometimes valuable pictures and antiques are found in the lofts of old houses."

"Wow," said Adam, "there might be a treasure chest up there!"

"I think that's a little unlikely," Jenny replied. "I understand treasure chests were usually left by smugglers and pirates, and even as the crow flies, we are over 25 miles from the sea! Still, we'll go up there and have a look. Now, you all need to be very sensible and very careful. I've only got the one torch, so do as I say, or we're coming straight back down. We cannot risk anyone falling through the ceiling. Are we all agreed?" All three children nodded their agreement. Jenny picked up the torch and went and collected the stepladder she had seen under the stairs and they all went upstairs to the landing.

Chapter 2
THE DAY BEFORE: THE MOVE

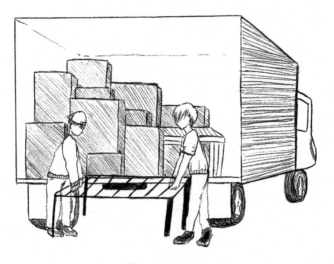

The moving van

The Jackson family had only moved into the old cottage the day before. It had been a tough 24 hours. They had left Hastings on Thursday, but hadn't arrived outside the cottage until midday on Friday. The moving van was already there when they arrived and the three moving men were leaning against the back of the van looking agitated, even annoyed. They had been waiting for Jenny for nearly half an hour. Jenny leaped out of the car and went to the front door of the cottage and unlocked it. Two of the men followed her in and asked her to stay in the hall, so she could say where each box was to go. Jenny and the children had arrived later than the moving van, as they had had to collect the keys from the estate agent in the Welsh village with an unpronounceable name.

Jenny had chosen this cottage on the estate agent's website. She hadn't even seen it in the flesh, taking a huge risk by instructing her solicitor to go ahead with the purchase.

Jack Jackson, her husband, had died two years ago and the last two years had been a terrible struggle. A few friends had rallied around the family, sadly not the ones they thought they could rely on, but the family had survived so far. In serious trouble, they had found out who their real friends were. With Jack's death, income virtually

Minafon Cottage

stopped. They had no life assurance or savings. The child benefit was the only payment Jenny continued to receive, so she had no chance of paying the mortgage. The building society, after months of threats to repossess the house, finally agreed to give her another year to sell the house and pay off the mortgage. Jenny thought that was only because she had children and the building society didn't want to be seen to be making the children homeless.

At first, Jenny was hoping Jack's employers would make a large payment in view of his death being an industrial accident on one of their building sites. The employer did look at the circumstances, but refused to help in any way. It appeared that Jack had been working on scaffolding three floors up and had lost concentration or become confused, as he'd stepped back without thinking and fallen to his death. The solicitor advised the employers that they shouldn't make any payment at all, as it could be viewed as an admission of liability in court. Jenny then went to the Citizens' Advice Bureau who told her she could get legal aid and could challenge the employer's decision, but on investigation there didn't appear to be any negligence on the part of the employer, so she was unlikely to win. That left Jenny with no other option than selling the house.

Once Jenny had a buyer for their house in Hastings, she started feverishly searching on all the 'houses for sale' websites for a cheap house. She had no income or job at present, so no-one was going to give her a mortgage, so she had to find a house she could afford to buy from the proceeds of the sale. Jenny finally found a cottage in Wales, advertised on a website for half the price of their house in Hastings. That meant they could pay off the mortgage and buy the cottage with cash. There were no other properties for sale with the right amount of accommodation for that price. If Jenny could get a job in that area, she had to take a chance on this cottage. Back on the websites she found a care home about a mile away from the cottage.

A phone call established the care home had a staff shortage and would be pleased to employ her as a care assistant. Jenny spoke to her solicitor and found out the cottage was vacant, as the owner had been an elderly lady who had passed away. Her daughter, who lived about two miles north of the Welsh village, had inherited the cottage but didn't want it, so she had put it up for sale. Jenny told her solicitor to go ahead with the sale and purchase the cottage, as it was the best deal they were likely to get.

The three children got out of the car and followed the moving men into the cottage. Katharine was the eldest at 15 years of age and was called Katie by everyone, including her mum. Jacqui, her sister, was 13 and their little brother, Adam, was 10. As the house seemed rather dark they waited in the hall next to Mum.

"The lights don't work," said Adam as he continued to flick the hall light switch on and off. Although it was midday and sunny outside, the hall was dark and gloomy. The walls were covered with dark red wallpaper and all the woodwork was brown. There was very little light coming in from outside. A small, opaque glass window in the front door let in a little light and the only other light came from the open door to the kitchen on the right-hand side of the hall. Jenny noticed the cupboard under the stairs and, opening it, managed to make out the fuse box. She pulled up the main electric switch and a dim, low voltage bulb hanging from the hall ceiling immediately glowed slightly, improving vision in the hall, but not by much. Since Jack's death, Jenny had had to become familiar with household electrics and plumbing fittings and controls.

The moving men went back out to the van and started to unload the furniture, boxes and suitcases that had come from their old house.

The family were referring to their previous house at Hastings, as their old house and this cottage as the new one, but Jenny found herself thinking that was weird. Their Hastings house had been about 40 years old, but this cottage was over 200 years old and looked every bit of it. Still, it was new to them. Now that Jenny had turned the electricity on, the children found the courage to start exploring their 'new' house, whilst Mum stayed in the hall directing the incoming beds and boxes.

Jenny shouted up the stairs, as the kids rushed up to choose the best bedrooms,

"There is supposed to be a double bedroom at the front of the house and that will be mine!"

Their dad, Jack, had worked on building sites since he had left school, but hadn't made much money, hence no private pension,

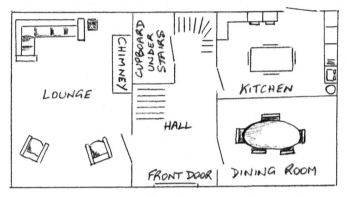

GROUND FLOOR PLAN OF COTTAGE

ADAM'S DRAWING WITH A LITTLE HELP FROM AMY RUSHTON

life assurance or savings. He had however been a hard worker and therefore never out of work, so the children were always well clothed and fed, and the mortgage was always paid on time. This had gone in their favour when arguing with the building society about repossession. Their transport though was a rather battered, high mileage Ford Focus, so their journey up from Hastings had been long and slow. They had had to spread it over two days, staying in a cheap motel last night. The moving van and crew had done the same, arriving just before them. After just an hour the men were closing the van's rear doors and wishing the family well. They were off, intending to be back in Hastings that day.

Jenny didn't have any valuable china or expensive furniture, but still hoped there wasn't any damage to their meagre possessions. The main thing was they were all there safe and sound, except of course for Dad, who was in every thought she had. Jenny found the heating controls and turned on the hot water and unpacked the food she had brought with them. She made them scrambled eggs and toast and lots of tea, whilst Jacqui and Adam opened the dining room curtains and set the old lady's table. Katie meanwhile found the box with the TV in it. It was a flat screen, but not one of those huge screens many people seem to have now. However, it did mean that it was light enough for Katie to carry to the lounge and she opened those curtains as well. She plugged the television into the mains and connected the aerial and then tried to tune it in, avoiding the Welsh-speaking channel.

She found BBC 1 and 2 which would do for now and went and joined the others eating scrambled eggs in the dining room.

Earlier, when the children had rushed upstairs, they found there wasn't much choice really as far as bedrooms were concerned. Mum had 'bags' on the front bedroom, which left two rear bedrooms, a double and a single. The two girls naturally took the big room, leaving the small room for Adam. A small room, Adam thought, but it is my own, not all bad at all. The old lady's daughter had sold the house with the contents, taking only Granny's personal items, but also the beds at Jenny's request. So, furniture-wise, the Jacksons hadn't brought much: a double bed, three single beds, a television and a dressing table, which Jenny had inherited from her mum and had sentimental value.

The moving men had put the double bed and dressing table in Jenny's room, two single beds in the other double room and Adam's bed in the single bedroom. Apart from the television which Katie had unpacked, everything else was in dozens of cardboard boxes and five suitcases spread around the house. Jenny opened the cardboard boxes that contained the bed linen and they all helped making up the beds. The rooms were all dark and gloomy; dark brown carpets, coloured flock wallpapers, heavy curtains and weak light bulbs. The house obviously hadn't been decorated for many, many years. With the lights working, it did help to make the place a little less scary. Nevertheless, Jenny was hoping that with all the travelling, the children would be in bed asleep before it was dark outside and sunset wasn't until 9 p.m. as it was the end of July.

"Katie," said Jenny, "don't worry about the dim lights; we'll get some 100-watt bulbs tomorrow. But for now, we need to concentrate on getting organised for tonight. Come with me and we'll check whose clothes are in what suitcase."

With that she led Katie upstairs and they started opening the suitcases. "This one's got Adam's clothes in. Take it to Adam's

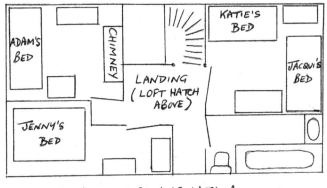

ADAM'S DRAWING WITH A
LITTLE HELP FROM THE AUTHOR

room and tell him to unpack the suitcase and put his clothes in a drawer, except his nightclothes, which should be on his bed." As Katie went off with Adam's case, Jenny started opening the other cases. Within a couple of hours, they all had their clothes put away in their rooms, except their nightwear, which lay waiting on their beds.

Later, Jenny got Katie tuning the TV again and eventually found a few more stations. They watched TV until Jenny gave them all a mug of hot tomato soup and tucked them up in bed. The children were so tired they fell asleep within minutes.

Chapter 3
THE LOFT

It was now late morning on Saturday and the family were standing upstairs on the landing. Whilst Jenny set up the stepladder, the three children gazed up at the loft hatch with high expectations in their eyes. But immediately Jenny set foot on the ladder, all three children took hold of it to keep it steady and safe for their mum. All three children had independently come to the realisation of the importance of helping Mum and keeping her safe. Having lost their dad, they now understood how fragile life could be and how even more important their mum was to them.

"Hang on to the torch for me Katie," said Jenny and very carefully climbed the ladder. At the top, she pushed the loft hatch lid up and back into the loft. They could all feel the cold, stale air from the loft opening and Jacqui shivered. Jenny noticed and wondered whether it was the cold air or if it was psychological, the thought of the cold, dark loft that no-one had been inside for several years. Jenny reached down for the torch from Katie and then moved up on to the top step of the ladder. Jenny's head was now through the hatch and, turning on the torch, she could see inside.

"Hey guys, we are in luck," Jenny said.

"What? Is there a treasure chest Mum?" Adam shouted, getting all excited.

"Not that I can see Adam. I mean we are in luck because the loft is boarded."

"Is that good Mum?" Adam asked.

"Absolutely Adam. It means we can climb up and walk around inside the loft and look at things."

Jenny carefully climbed up through the hatch opening into the loft and shone the torch around, and at once spotted a switch. Flicking the switch down, a light bulb immediately came on. It was hanging from the roof, about halfway along the loft, near the chimney. Wow, Jenny thought, a bit more luck. The children could see the light in the loft, but it was so weak they just assumed it was Jenny's torch. Jenny was on her knees on the floorboards and leant down, sticking her head out of the loft hatch.

"Katie, you saw where I put the spare bulbs. Find the new 100-watt one, it's still in its box, and bring it up to me please."

"Okay," she said and hurried down the stairs. A couple of minutes later Katie reappeared and climbed up the ladder and passed the bulb to her mum. Jenny turned off the light in the loft and using her torchlight, changed the bulb for the new one. The old bulb was now hot, so Jenny had had to remove it using a hankie from her trouser pocket. She passed the hot bulb, still wrapped in the hankie, down to Katie.

"Be careful Katie, that bulb is hot."

"It's okay Mum, I'll put it in the cupboard with the others."

When Katie returned, Jenny said to her, "Help Adam up the ladder and I'll help him into the loft. Then do the same with

Jenny climbing up to the loft

Jacqui and you come in behind her. Adam, I know you won't want to be left out, so you must be very careful."

Within a few minutes the whole family were standing in the loft. Jenny thought it looked as though the whole loft was boarded, although she couldn't be sure until they had thoroughly examined it. The loft was quite large, spanning the entire cottage, but was very, very dirty. Now the stronger light bulb was shining, they could see the hundreds of spiderwebs and layers of dust. Underneath them were piles of old, tatty furniture that looked as though they had passed their 'sell-by date' 200 years ago and probably had.

"Right," said Jenny, "you guys can explore, but there are two rules. Firstly, you have to hold hands. Katie and Jacqui you are together and Adam is with me. That's because we don't know if there are any holes in the floorboards or even if the boarding will carry our weight."

"What's the second rule Mum?" asked Jacqui.

"You don't actually touch anything," Jenny replied.

"Oh Muum! So what's the point?" Adam complained.

"We are just going to look around this time," Jenny replied. "Mainly to check the flooring covers the whole loft and it will take our weight. If all's okay, we'll come back up here tomorrow with the vacuum cleaner and suck up a lot of the dust and spiders. We can then start to have a proper search."

They walked carefully around the loft, Jenny using her torch and trying hard to see the flooring at the sides and corners. The three ladies had to be careful not to bump their heads and had to keep ducking under the wooden joists in the roof. Adam had no such problem, as he was just short enough to walk around unheeded. After a while Jenny was fairly happy the flooring covered the whole loft and seemed to be made of strong boards that bore their weight without a problem. She called a halt to their loft inspection and helped the children out of the loft and back down the ladder. She switched off the loft light, closed the hatch and returned the ladder to the cupboard under the stairs.

Jenny had brought a large bag of potatoes with them from their old house and decided to cook baked potatoes with baked beans and they ate them watching the television. Afterwards, she remembered that last night, when she couldn't sleep, she had noticed a reading light on the wall above her headboard. She had also noticed that it didn't have a light bulb. She took one of the spare bulbs up to her bedroom and fitted it. Hey presto, it worked. The bulb was one of the old weak ones, but it was perfect for a reading light. Staying in her room, she finished her unpacking and then went around the house tidying up and cleaning. Adam had found pencils and paper in one of the cardboard boxes and was entertaining himself by drawing floor plans of the cottage. Later that evening, Jenny made everyone soup and bread, after which, they were all happy to go to bed. They were all tired, still suffering from the house move.

Jenny in the loft

Chapter 4
THE HUMMING NOISE RETURNS

Jenny had opened her one and only bottle of wine; a red wine, a pinotage from South Africa. She had been saving it to celebrate the successful house move. She hadn't envisaged drinking it alone, but right now she wanted a glass of wine and felt she deserved it. After getting the children comfortable in their beds, she got ready for the night, turned on her reading light and climbed into bed with a paperback novel and her glass of wine. As she read her book she sipped her wine and eventually realised she had drunk the whole glass. In a minute, she thought, she would get up and fetch another glass of wine; but for now, she returned to the book.

Suddenly there was a knock on her

bedroom door, it opened and Adam stuck his head around the door. She must have fallen asleep; the reading light was still on. She was very glad she had finished her glass of wine, as the glass was lying on its side on the duvet. If that wine had spilled, it would have stained her bed linen. Jenny was still half asleep.

"What's the problem Adam?" Jenny drowsily asked.

"I can't sleep Mummy. I could see you had your light on, I thought you were awake. There's a noise above me, I think it comes from the loft." Jenny shook her head to wake up and then listened. Sure enough, it was the same noise that had disturbed her last night.

I must find out what that is and fix it if I can, she thought. "Are the girls still awake Adam?"

"Don't think so Mummy, they were talking earlier but their room is quiet now."

"Okay," said Jenny, "climb in next to me."

Adam happily got in next to his mum and cuddled up close to her. Within minutes

Adam had fallen asleep, but Jenny lay there listening to the strange noise. It wasn't blowing a gale outside like last night. In fact, there didn't seem to be a breath of wind. The old cottage was quiet, no creaks and groans, which made the humming noise seem much louder. It also seemed like the noise was more demanding, even calling.

She started thinking about the rumours that the old lady was a witch but quickly dismissed those thoughts; she was going to give herself nightmares! The noise was weird though. It wasn't a groan or creak, like old houses make, it was a hum. Like a large bee or an electrical appliance, but nothing she could identify. It really was as though the noise was calling out to them. It was hard to ignore but she was still very tired and snuggled down and cuddled Adam, and quickly fell back to sleep.

The next morning Jenny told the children to put on their old T-shirts and jeans.

"Before we climb up to the loft and get dirty, I want us all to have a good breakfast," Jenny said. "We have come a long way in the last two years and I don't just mean from Hastings. We have pulled together as a family and your dad would be proud of you. As well as cereal, I'm going to make us eggs and toast. Enjoy it. It won't be every day, I'm afraid."

After breakfast, Jenny told Katie and Jacqui to go through the boxes and find the vacuum cleaner and extension lead.

"Adam, you can clear up the breakfast things, bring them into the kitchen and help me wash the dishes."

The children were happy to help Mum, it had been a great breakfast and they were all still excited by the prospect of the search in the loft. Adam was convinced he was going to find a treasure chest. Between them they took the vacuum cleaner, extension lead, stepladder and torch up to the landing. It was a real struggle getting the vacuum cleaner up into the loft, but they got it there eventually.

With the new, stronger light bulb they could see in the loft fairly well. Jenny's plan was to start hoovering from one end of the loft, above the girls' room and bathroom, and work slowly towards the other end where there was much more clutter, above her bedroom and Adam's room. It was fun sucking up all the spiders and webs, although Jenny decided to immediately empty the cleaner outside the cottage when she'd finished. The thought of all those spiders climbing back out would affect her sleep again.

As she hoovered up the spiders and the worst of the dust, the children examined the clutter. It was mostly old furniture and cardboard boxes, some of which were sealed. It was going to take days to clean and search the whole loft.

Still, Jenny thought, *we have made a start.* By mid-afternoon they all had had enough of the dirt and grime, and they came down from the loft. They left the vacuum cleaner and extension up there, just bringing down the cleaner bag for emptying, together with the torch. Jenny had no idea how reliable the lights of the cottage were and if they fused she would have a big problem if the torch was in the loft. The stepladder was left on the landing.

The family were all filthy and Jenny was very aware she was starting her new job tomorrow and had to be there at 7.30 in the morning, as it was her first day. She still had to organise her papers, her clothes for the morning and packed lunch, but first she needed to make a meal as everyone was hungry. Whilst Jenny cooked up sausage and mash, they all took it in turns to have a bath and put their clothes in the linen basket. It was a quiet night again except for the humming noise. Jenny didn't know if they were getting used to it, but it didn't keep anyone awake. They all slept well and Jenny was up and out of the house by 7 a.m., telling Katie she had made sandwiches for them for lunch and that Katie must make sure she kept a close eye on the other two.

"Especially Adam," said Jenny. "You know what he is like. He'll do anything to stop being bored. Katie, you must remember, you are the adult while I'm away. I have total trust in you, so act responsibly and keep an eye on and control the others. You've got the care home's number if there's a problem. I checked our phone and it is now working." She kissed them all and rushed out of the house.

Chapter 5

THE SEARCH FOR THE TREASURE CHEST

All three children were now awake and out of bed. They slowly made their way into the kitchen where they found the cereal bowls on the table. Next to the bowls were the cornflakes' packet, toaster and bread. No eggs that morning. Katie put the kettle on for tea and they had breakfast in front of the television. Adam seemed to suddenly light up.

"Hey guys, why don't we go and search for this treasure chest?"

"Adam," replied Katie, "there is no treasure chest. Mum is just going along with you to get you to help and keep you interested."

"You don't know that! What if there is one?" he shouted. Katie sat and thought about it.

The Children start to explore the loft

Well, she thought, *we haven't got anything else to do, so we might as well look for treasure chests.* "Okay, after breakfast we get old clothes on and go up into the loft again. Just remember though, Mum has put me in charge and what I say goes. Anyone acting like an idiot and we stop and come back down. Okay?" Katie said, looking hard at Adam. Jacqui and Adam both nodded. They continued their breakfast, but Adam was very excited and nearly choked twice as he didn't stop talking. Once they had finished breakfast, they went upstairs and dressed.

The stepladder was still on the landing, so Katie opened the ladder out and climbed up, pushing the loft hatch lid back into the loft. Ignoring the cold draft of air from the loft, Katie climbed up inside. She found the light switch in the dark and flicked it on. The new bright bulb filled the loft with light and Katie told the others to climb up.

"Jacqui, let Adam come up next, so you can help him if necessary."

Adam might have been only 10 years of

age and shorter than his big sisters, but he was strong for his size, and climbed up into the loft with ease. Once they were all safely in the loft, Katie had decided to put the loft hatch lid back into its hole. That way, if one of them stepped back without thinking, they wouldn't fall out of the loft. She was impressed with herself for thinking of that.

Without even discussing it, the children split up, each going to different parts of the loft. They were pulling out items of furniture and examining them, looking in drawers and opening boxes. It all looked like it hadn't been disturbed for many, many years. Then without warning there was a terrible scream from Jacqui. A big spider had come out of hiding and run on to her exploring hand. Adam quickly ran over to Jacqui and flicked the spider off her hand. It ran off into a dark corner of the loft. After two hours of searching they had found lots of old books and a few old children's toys that must have been put away for sentimental reasons. So far, they had found nothing to get excited about, apart from the spider of course.

Then all three of them screamed as there was a 'ping' noise and they were plunged into total darkness.

"Oh hell!" shouted Adam. Katie didn't tell him off, as she had nearly said something much worse.

"Okay," said Katie, recovering first, "I think it's just the bulb that has blown."

"But that's a new bulb," Jacqui pointed out.

"It is, but maybe it had been dropped or was faulty. I don't know," Katie replied. "We mustn't panic. We must just stay quiet and still. Don't move around. I didn't think to bring up the torch. I'll feel for the loft hatch and carefully open it. That'll give us light to climb down and get the torch and another bulb."

"Wait a minute Katie," shouted Adam, "be quiet and listen. There's that noise again." They stopped talking and listened, and sure enough there was that humming noise that Jenny and Adam had been hearing at night, but this time it was much louder.

"That noise wasn't there before the light

went out," said Jacqui.

"No, it wasn't," agreed Katie. "What are you saying Adam? Have you heard it before?"

"It's been keeping me awake at night and Mum hates it as well. I guess you guys can't hear it in your bedroom," Adam replied. "Mum didn't actually say anything to me, but I know she wants to find out where that noise is coming from."

"It won't be safe for us to explore in the dark," said Katie. "But I'll tell you what I am going to do. I'm going to get on my knees and find that loft hatch lid and open it. With luck the noise will continue, but there'll be enough light to find out where it is coming from. You guys just stay calm and don't move a muscle."

With that Katie got down on her knees and started crawling towards where she thought the loft hatch was. As she carefully searched, she told Jacqui and Adam to stay quiet, concentrate on the noise and try and judge what direction it came from. As Katie crawled along and slowly searched the loft flooring with her hands, she suddenly thought of all the spiders in the loft! She quickly put the thought out of her mind otherwise she was going to lose it and panic.

Then her hands hit something, but when she felt the shape of it she realised it was the vacuum cleaner they had left up there. She'd forgotten all about it. She carried on moving towards where she thought the hatch was. Then she noticed a square of light and realised it was the light from the landing, shining around the edges of the hatch lid. She found the raised frame that enclosed the hatch and then she felt inside the frame where she could see the light along the edges of the hatch lid and carefully raised it up and lent it against a box. There was now light, not much, but they weren't in total darkness.

"Well," said Katie, "can you still hear the noise?" But as she asked the question, she realised she could hear it, so stood up and started walking towards the sound. It seemed to be coming from the chimney, which came up through the centre of the loft. The three children moved slowly towards the chimney, concentrating on the sound, as though they were approaching a distressed fledgling and were scared it would fly away if they frightened it. The humming was definitely louder here by the chimney.

Katie was about to say it must be inside the chimney when Adam pointed at the chimney and shouted, "Look there! Look at those bricks! They've got an orange glow around them! It looks like there is a light behind those three bricks." The other two came closer to the chimney.

"Wow! You're right," said Jacqui.

Katie had made a quick plan in her head.

"Listen you two. I want you both to stay here and stay looking at those bricks, so we can identify them if the glowing light stops. I think this is significant. I'm going down the ladder to get the torch, a bulb, a screwdriver and a piece of chalk."

"Why the screwdriver and chalk, Katie?" asked Adam.

"For the bricks, silly," said Jacqui.

"Hey Jacqui, don't call your brother silly!" rebuked Katie. "You are right though," she said to Jacqui. With that Katie made her way to the hatch and climbed down the ladder.

Katie, the older sister

Chapter 6
THE DISCOVERY

Katie found the torch in the kitchen and took a light bulb from the cupboard, but knew the screwdriver and chalk would be more of a problem. She remembered her dad's toolbox and hoped it was in one of the cardboard boxes in the lounge. As well as tools, such as hammers and screwdrivers, he also used to have pieces of chalk in the top tray of his toolbox and Katie guessed they would still be there. She went to the pile of unopened cardboard boxes and ended up opening seven of them before she found the toolbox. Sure enough there were several sticks of chalk in the top tray of the toolbox and she took one, together with a large screwdriver. She left the top of the toolbox open. That would remind her to put them back.

Back up in the loft, Katie found Adam

leaning against the chimney, his hand resting on the three bricks. She could clearly hear the humming noise and an orange light was still visible around the bricks that Adam had his hand on. With Jacqui holding the torch, Katie marked big crosses with the chalk on all three bricks and then changed the light bulb for the one she had brought up from the kitchen. She knew it wouldn't be very bright, as it was one of the old bulbs left by the previous owner. It did work, but the strangest thing happened. After changing the bulb, when Katie turned the light back on, both the humming noise and the orange light immediately stopped. In the improved light, they could now see each other and they all looked nervous and worried. There was now this deathly silence.

What was going on? they all thought.

"We've come this far," Katie said, "are you guys okay?"

Jacqui nodded and Adam said, "You bet. It's just beginning to get interesting."

So, Katie picked up the screwdriver and

started to push it in around the bricks with the chalk crosses where the light had been coming from. There were three bricks with crosses on in the middle of the chimney stack. They were unusually directly above each other and not staggered as one would expect. They were normal-sized house bricks, about eight inches long and two and a half inches high. Jacqui had turned the torch back on and was pointing it at the bricks giving Katie better light. After a couple of minutes one of the bricks moved and Katie was able to start easing it out of the chimney breast. Two minutes later the brick was loose and was sticking out enough for Katie to get hold of it. She looked at Jacqui and then Adam.

"Okay?" she said. They both nodded and Katie pulled the brick right out of the chimney. Nothing further happened. Katie turned the brick around in her hand whilst Jacqui shone the torch on it, but it was just a brick. She put it down on the loft floor. Now, the other two bricks came out more easily. This made a dark hole in the side of the chimney breast about eight inches square.

Then Adam snatched the torch from Jacqui, who shouted, "Hey! What the hell?" But Adam was pointing the torch into the hole in the chimney, where the bricks had come from. It appeared to be only a black hole. There was no light, or bulb, or anything that could have caused the orange light. The hole looked empty.

As Adam put his hand into the hole Katie shouted, "Adam, I don't think that's safe!"

"It's okay Katie, the hole's empty," he said, very disappointed.

"I can't believe that," Jacqui said. "That humming noise brought us up into the loft. That orange light brought us to these bricks. It's like magic!" As she said this, Jacqui moved forward, to see into the hole for herself.

Adam gave Jacqui the torch back and stepped back out of her way. However, as he did so, his head touched something, so he snatched the torch back. He shone the torch upwards to see what it was that had touched his head because he was scared it was another big spider. Jacqui was about to protest because he had snatched the torch back yet again, but then realised the beam of the torch was lighting up a key, hanging from a hook.

"Listen guys," said Jacqui, "this is more magic. These roof beams are about five feet from the floor, everyone has to duck under them except you Adam. You, Adam, can just walk around the loft without hitting your head. That key, however, is exactly at the height for it to touch your head so we find it. Call it coincidence, call it magic, but that key must be there for a reason. So what does it fit?"

As she was the tallest, Katie stretched across and took the torch from Adam and stepped in front of the hole. Holding the torch with her left hand, she put her right hand into the hole. The hole was only 4 inches deep, the width of a brick. But the back of the hole didn't feel like brick, it was smooth, like metal. She pushed it and it moved a fraction. Feeling around it she found a very small hole. She took her hand out and shining the torch inside, she could see the end of the hole and it was obvious that there was a small vertical, metal door in the back of the hole. It was about six inches square and similar to the type of door often seen on a small house safe. Katie thought that the small hole in the metal door looked like a keyhole, and reached over and took the key off the hook. The key fitted into the keyhole and she was able to turn it. As she did so, the metal door inside the hole swung open towards her. With the aid of the torch, she could now see through the open door and what looked like a small roll of cardboard inside.

"Hey guys. This wall must be two bricks thick, because there is a safe in here, with a roll of cardboard or paper in it," Katie said.

"Well?" cried Adam. "Is it a treasure map?" Telling Adam to keep calm, she put her hand back inside and pulled out the roll. Adam went to snatch it from her, but Katie very quickly pulled it away.

"Adam, for heaven's sake!" she yelled at him. "You'll tear it! Just wait a minute."

"But I'm right, aren't I? It's bound to be a treasure map. It'll tell us where the treasure is!" Adam shouted, getting more and more excited.

Katie calmly moved so she was under the light bulb and slowly and carefully unrolled what turned out to be a scroll of very old paper. Jacqui had moved next to her and was trying to look over Katie's shoulder. Adam was nearly jumping up and down.

Katie looked at Adam and Jacqui and said, "It looks like it is some sort of clue, like you get on a treasure hunt, so you could actually be right, Adam."

"There you are!" he screamed. "I told you so!"

"Adam," said Katie, "I said it could be, not that it definitely was. Stay calm. We'll see."

"I can't see it that well," said Jacqui. "What does it say?"

Katie was still looking at the scroll of old paper, so read it aloud;

"Upon the stone above the Tyr,
Lies the clue that takes you there."

Upon the stone above the Tyr,

Lies the clue that takes you there.

The Children find the first Clue

"What the heck does that mean?" Jacqui asked.

"I don't have any idea," Katie replied. "We'll go downstairs, have some tea and try and work it out."

Chapter 7
THE FIRST CLUE

When they got back downstairs Katie went into the kitchen and put the kettle on. Then the three of them had tea and the sandwiches their mum had left for them, while they talked about the clue. Adam was bubbling with excitement and couldn't wait to tell Mum. Katie was quiet and listening, and thinking about it all.

"I think we need to think about this and make careful plans," said Katie.

"Yeah, you're right," said Jacqui. "If we tell Mum she'll go berserk. She won't let us follow the clue on our own and with Mum's new job, she won't have time to come with us or help us for days."

"I agree, we mustn't tell Mum. In fact, we mustn't tell anyone. We are going to have to solve the clue and follow it up, all on our own," Katie replied. "Now listen carefully Adam," Katie continued, "we can see you are very excited, but if you say a word to Mum or anyone else, we'll have to show the clue to others and it won't be our treasure hunt any more. We found the clue, so we don't tell anyone and we follow it up ourselves. Are we all in agreement?"

Jacqui and Adam both agreed.

"Okay then. First thing we do is go back up to the loft and put everything back as it was. That means the little metal door is closed, the bricks go back into the hole and the chalk and screwdriver go back into Dad's toolbox. The stepladder was on the landing, but it must be exactly in the same place. There mustn't be anything different to make Mum think we've been in the loft."

"Then we need to get rid of the crosses on the bricks," Adam said.

"That's easy," Jacqui replied. "We turn them around the other way and put the sides with the crosses in first."

"And what do we say when Mum asks us what we've been doing all day?" Katie asked.

"Homework," Jacqui replied, with a loud groan from Adam. "You know it makes sense. We all have homework for the summer holiday and it's got to be done. If we do some this afternoon, it'll mean we haven't left it all for the end of the holiday and Mum will be pleased," Jacqui continued.

"When I came down to find the chalk and a screwdriver," Katie said, "I ended up opening seven of the boxes and leaving the toolbox open as well. As you haven't got much homework Adam, maybe you can help me. We can close up the toolbox and empty the other cardboard boxes and put things away. Mum would love that too."

By the time Jenny got home, it was nearly 8.30 in the evening. The care home was struggling with staff shortages, so Jenny had agreed to do four 12-hour shifts for that week and the next. The care home had given her the next two weekends off, but it meant for the next two weeks she was doing 48 hours a week! The truth was that Jenny was so short of money she wasn't so much helping the care home out, as getting money the family desperately needed. Nevertheless, whilst the rest of the care home staff were doing 36 hours a week, that is three days a week, Jenny was doing four days a week!

Jenny came into the cottage totally shattered and collapsed into a chair. She seriously wondered if she could work all these hours. However, when she found out how much homework the children had done, she was so pleased, the tiredness seemed to fall away. She made soup and buttered some bread and they ate the last of the cherry cake. A neighbour in Hastings had given it to the family as a farewell present, which was very much appreciated.

"I've made a list of things we need and you'll be really helping me out if you go to the shop tomorrow to get them," Jenny said. "You must all go together and stay together all the time. I've written down directions to the village shop and here's the money Katie. Please be very careful, with each other and with the money. I don't get paid for two whole weeks."

When Jenny went up to have a bath, the children continued their discussion of what the clue meant. They didn't know what a Tyr was and still had no ideas at all. Still, they had all agreed they couldn't ask anyone, so were hoping for inspiration. They went to bed none the wiser. Jenny slept like a log. She hadn't noticed there wasn't any humming from the loft. She had been so tired she fell asleep as her head hit the pillow. The children were also very tired, but were excited and couldn't stop thinking about the clue. They did eventually fall asleep.

At a quarter to eight in the morning Jenny kissed them all, told them she loved them and told them to be sensible, careful and look after each other. They all promised they would and said they loved her. Jenny rushed out of the cottage. After they finished dressing and having some breakfast, they decided to go to the shop and 'get it over with'. They would then be able to concentrate on the clue.

They walked down to the village with

Katie holding the money and their mum's directions. The directions were not really necessary. There was only one junction in the road and as long as they turned left and didn't follow the village signs they would arrive at the shop. The children had been to the village shop before, but only once and then in the car, so Jenny thought they might not have noticed the route. As they approached the road junction Adam cried out, like he'd been stung by a wasp. The others turned and froze.

"What's the matter Adam?" Katie called.

"Look, just look at the village sign!" Adam screamed.

"Well," Katie replied, "it just says 'CWMTYR', that's the village's name I guess," and then the penny dropped. "Heck, I see what you mean Adam. The second part of the village's name is TYR."

"Exactly Katie!" Adam shouted.

"Brilliant, well noticed Adam. If that's the name of the village, it won't seem strange at all for us newcomers to ask about the name. We'll go to the shop as planned and

I'll casually ask about the name," Katie said, very pleased with her plan.

The Village sign

At the shop, they bought their groceries and as they were ready to leave Katie turned back and casually asked about the name of the village, its pronunciation and meaning.

The lady shopkeeper said, "It's two Welsh words. The first word is Cwm (pronounced 'coom') and means valley and the second is Tyr (pronounced 'tear') and is the name of the river. So, the name of the village is 'Valley of the river Tyr.'"

"Okay, thank you very much," said Katie and they all left the shop with smiles on their faces.

Chapter 8
FOLLOW THE RIVER

They were on their way back to the cottage when they passed an elderly man walking towards them.

Jacqui said, "Bore da," as he came close.

He must have heard her English accent or realised they were not locals because he said, "Good morning to you," in reply.

Jacqui stopped dead, realising he spoke English and he was also friendly.

"Can I ask you something sir?" she said, showing respect for his age.

"Yes, my dear. What's the problem?"

"Well sir, we are new here, just moved in. We are on our school summer break and my little brother here loves to fish. We've been told there is a river Tyr, but don't know how to find it. Can you help us?"

"Where do you live?" he said.

"We can't answer that question sir,"

Jacqui replied. "Our mum says we mustn't give personal details to a stranger and made us promise we would stay safe."

"Your mother is very sensible and so are you by obeying her. So let me answer your question another way. I know everyone around here and I hear an English family have moved into the old cottage a mile up the road. In front of that old cottage is a sign which says *'Minafon'*. It is Welsh and is pronounced minervon, which means by the river," he replied. "Whether you live in that cottage or not, the river you seek runs behind that very cottage."

They all thanked the man for his help and turned to walk away.

Then suddenly Katie turned around and called to the man, who was now walking away from them.

"Excuse me sir!" she called. "Can I ask one last question?"

"Yes, of course," the man said. "How can I help?"

"I just remembered we were told to fish off the bridge. Is there an old stone bridge over the river?"

"Certainly, there is; about one mile upstream of that cottage."

"Thank you again, you've been very helpful," Katie said and had a big grin on her face as she walked away.

When they got back to the cottage, Jacqui and Adam put away the shopping, whilst Katie made the tea and then the three of them sat around the table to plan the treasure hunt. Katie had the paper with the clue on it, laid out on the table:

'Upon the stone above the Tyr,
Lies the clue that takes you there.'

"I think I understand the clue now," Katie said. "As you now know, the Tyr is the local river that runs behind this house. One mile upstream of the river is a stone bridge. I think it is a fair bet that there is a stone in the centre of the bridge and on this stone we will find the next clue. We have to follow the river and find this bridge."

"Wow Katie," said Adam. "That's really

Jacqui, the younger sister

brilliant of you. So, what are we waiting for? Let's go!"

"No Adam. It is a mile up the river. It will take a long time to walk that. Remember, we will be walking across country and of course we must be home safe, before Mum returns. Before you groan Adam, we must do some more homework this afternoon, so Mum is happy and then get everything ready. Tomorrow we leave immediately after Mum goes to work, so we have the whole day to find this next clue."

"What do we need to get ready?" Jacqui asked.

"We need to pack our backpacks with a bottle of water, sandwiches, notepad and pen, the care home's telephone number, screwdriver and hammer, money, some spare clothes, the torch and Mum's little digital camera. We'll need to find the camera and check it's got batteries," Katie replied.

"Wow Katie," said Jacqui, "you've really thought about this. Why do we need all that stuff?"

"Water to drink, sandwiches to eat, notepad to write down the clue when we find it, the care home's number in case we get into trouble, tools in case we have to dig out the stone, torch in case it's in a dark place, spare clothes in case someone falls in the river, some money for emergencies and a camera to record anything exciting we find," explained Katie.

"You really have thought about this," Jacqui replied.

"Yes, I have," Katie said. "But we need to check something for tomorrow morning, before Mum gets home. Come with me the two of you." With that Katie went to the back door and opened it and went through, taking the key. Once the other two were also outside, Katie closed the door and put the key in and locked it.

"Okay," she said, "the door does lock from the outside. Now let's find out if there's a gate at the end of the garden and if we can get out that way."

The three of them did find a gate at the end of the garden, it wasn't locked and they did manage to wrestle it open. The garden had not had any attention for many years, with the grass up to their knees and stinging nettles and thistles everywhere. But there was an old pathway to the back gate and although it was badly overgrown, it was still useable with careful avoidance of the nettles, thistles and the thorns of the wild roses.

"Okay," said Katie. "I just needed to know if we could get out this way. So, let's do some homework and pack our backpacks and hide them under our beds."

When Jenny got home, she was again totally shattered, but was also amazed about the children having done some more homework, without her there to nag them. She was also pleased that they had done the shopping, which meant she was able to make them all spaghetti bolognaise, Adam's favourite. Katie told her mum that they were all worried about her having to do such long hours, so they were 'trying to do their bit'. Jenny accepted that and didn't become suspicious. The three children were bathed and in bed by 10 p.m. The two girls whispered in bed about their plans for a whole hour, before going to sleep, whilst Adam, in his own room, dreamed of al the treasure they were going to find.

Chapter 9
THEY MEET 'NOOGAN'

As planned, they had secretly packed their two backpacks, so that when Jenny left, they were ready to go immediately. Jenny kissed them all goodbye, told Adam and Jacqui to obey Katie and told Katie to 'be the adult', look after them and make sure they all stayed safe.

"Ring me at work if you have any problems or worries. I mean it! I'd prefer to know if there was a problem, even if it's one you think you can handle." With that Jenny kissed them all and rushed out of the cottage.

"You know what?" Katie said to Jacqui. "I keep thinking she knows all about the treasure hunt. The way Mum kept telling me to take charge, to keep you guys safe and to ring her if we had any worries!"

"No, she can't know or she'd be going

crazy," Jacqui replied. "But she probably does know we are up to something, she just doesn't know what. Come on then, we need to make tracks, as they say."

The weather looked changeable, so all three had put on hoodies, even though it was nearly August. They were now in Wales, of course, and had no experience of Welsh weather, so, as Katie had pointed out, better be safe than sorry. The girls put on their backpacks and the three of them left. They went out of the back door, locking it behind them and down the garden, and with a struggle, through the gate at the end.

Behind the cottage, the ground sloped downwards, into a valley. In places, the heather and grasses came up to their waists and they quickly realised they had to step forward very carefully as the ground was very uneven. There were also stones and rocks everywhere and hurrying through this terrain would be very foolish, they could easily twist an ankle. They stepped carefully and slowly down the slope, towards the valley, away from the rear of the garden.

After about 20 minutes they heard the sound of running water, which immediately made them feel a little more confident.

"We don't know how big this river is or how deep it is, so we must be especially careful," Katie said. Jacqui and Adam agreed and said they would take care.

Jacqui then said, "The great thing about following the river is we can't get lost. At any time, we can turn around and be sure of the way back. However guys, we must make sure we can recognise this bit of the river, so we know where to leave the river and go uphill to find our cottage."

"That was a very clever and very sensible comment Jacqui," Katie responded. "We'll do just that. Come on, stop and turn and look up the hill. Try and remember something that will enable us to find the cottage on our return." The three of them stopped and tried to find something they would easily recognise again.

A few more minutes of careful downward walking and they found the river, more of a stream really. It wasn't very big and was probably only about two-feet deep. They turned right and followed it upstream, after again making sure they would recognise that spot when they returned. They walked along the top of the bank as it was less of a struggle than through the undergrowth, but the going was still very slow. The river ran through the valley, between rocks and fields with long grass and loads of tall thistles! There was a wood ahead and they noticed that the river ran from the centre of the wood.

This didn't however deter Adam at all. He was so excited with the treasure hunt that he kept trying to hurry on ahead. He was ignoring Katie and Jacqui, who were shouting at him to stay with them. Even though Adam was the smallest of the three, Katie and Jacqui were struggling to keep up with him on this difficult terrain, especially as they were carrying the backpacks. At the entrance to the woods the going became easier and Adam hurried into the woods, despite Katie shouting for him to wait for them. When they lost sight of Adam the girls became very nervous. They both started to run into the wood, calling out his name, trying to catch up with him.

They ran between the trees, the way they thought Adam had gone and came upon a small clearing in the wood. They both suddenly stopped and froze to the spot. There in front of them was Adam's back. He was standing completely still and looking at a strange, small man. The small man was definitely not a child, but was only the same height as Adam. He was grotesque to look at with huge ears and nose, a bald head and staring eyes. He had hands and feet like claws and spindly legs. His legs reminded Katie of an ostrich she had seen at a zoo. He was wearing strange clothes, as though he was a pirate, and held a staff in his right claw.

He opened his mouth and said in a deep guttural voice, "I am called 'Noogan'. I know you are looking for 'Sofire'. I am a friend of hers. I need to tell you to be quiet and gentle when you meet her. Do not shout or frighten her. She is nice and won't

They meet Noogan

hurt you, but she is very dangerous if made angry. Show her respect and you'll be fine."

Katie had never seen anything like this creature and grabbed her mum's camera out of her bag. She put the camera to her eye but couldn't see the creature in the viewfinder. She lowered the camera and he wasn't there. He seemed to have just disappeared! Jacqui and Adam were standing there, totally silent.

"Where has he gone?" said Katie.

Eventually Jacqui said, "He just, sort of, faded away!" Jacqui was obviously stunned and virtually speechless.

Katie nervously looked around her. She didn't know what she was looking for and she thought to herself, *Nothing right now is normal and nothing makes sense.*

"The bad news guys," Katie said to the others, "is that everything has gone crazy. We are surrounded by some form of magic. A funny noise called us up into the loft, a strange orange light led us to a clue and now some magical creature is giving us advice we never asked for. And who the heck is 'Sofire'? However, the good news is that everything appears to be trying to help us. The noise, the orange light and even this weird creature are all helping us. I don't think we are in danger. Are you two happy to carry on with the treasure hunt?"

Katie had hardly got the words out and Adam screamed, "Yes. Yes of course. This is the best!"

"I agree," said Jacqui. "If we stopped now, we would spend the rest of our lives wondering what we would have found."

"Okay, we need to go silently," Katie said. "We need to listen for the river and go back to the riverbank. We mustn't get lost in this wood."

Once they stopped talking, the children heard the running water and made their way back to the riverbank. They continued to follow the river upstream, as planned, but they kept looking around themselves, expecting another creature to turn up at any moment. The going was slow as there still wasn't a path next to the riverbank and there were several times they had to navigate around thick, impenetrable bushes or beds of stinging nettles. Also, the longer they spent in the wood, the more they had the feeling of not being alone. They kept thinking they saw something, or someone, moving behind them. They were beginning to think they were being followed. Even Adam had lost the spring in his step and was getting jumpy.

Jacqui was just beginning to wonder if the stone bridge really existed, when they realised the trees were thinning out and then, shortly afterwards, the wood came to an end. Katie, Jacqui and Adam found themselves standing at the edge of a field. Walking through the wood, worrying and being distracted about being followed, they had wandered to the right. The river was now about a hundred yards to their left. In the field in front of them was a crop of wheat, that looked like it was ready for harvesting.

The Children come out of the wood

At the other side of the field they could see the top of a hedge, running from right to left, where it met a bridge. It looked like a stone bridge and they assumed that on the other side of the hedge was a country road which went over the bridge. They knew that the river was on their left as they had been following it and it was a reasonable assumption that it went under the bridge.

"I guess that's our bridge guys," Jacqui said.

"Well it looks like stone, at least from here," replied Katie.

"So why are we talking about it? Let's go and see if the clue is right!" Adam shouted.

Chapter 10
MAGIC, SCARY OR JUST WEIRD?

Adam was about to walk into the field of wheat when Katie grabbed his arm.

"Adam, you know better than that. Remember whenever we went into the country, Dad would always say to us the two rules. Always close gates that were closed when you got to them and never walk across a field that has a crop in it. That's wheat Adam and you'll do terrible damage to it by walking across it. As well as that, it's nearly four-feet high, ready for harvest, and you would hardly be able to see where you're going. Come on, we'll walk around the edge of the field. Any rate, it'll probably be quicker."

So the three of them turned left towards the river and walked next to the wheat field. At the corner of the field they turned right and started heading towards the bridge. The wheat field was on their right and firstly Adam, and then Jacqui, became aware of lots of rustling sounds in the field. Then Katie too found herself looking at the field, wondering what the noises were. Katie, being taller than the other two, could see the top of the wheat was moving and this movement appeared to be keeping up with them, as they walked along. Katie was just beginning to get the idea they were being followed, when she suddenly saw what could only be a bald head.

"Hey, you!" she shouted. "Show yourself. What are you doing in there?"

Almost immediately a head popped up and stared at them. The three children jumped. Even though they had known something was going on, they never expected this head to actually appear! The head was weird. Similar to the creature that had surprised them in the wood; it had a bald head and a huge nose and ears. It also had big eyes and seemed to be continuously staring at them.

"What are you? What are you doing?" Katie demanded.

"I'm Kittle," it said, in a type of guttural voice, similar to the previous creature. This one was less scary though. Maybe because they had already seen one of these creatures they weren't so shocked, or maybe it was because this one looked gentler, even cute.

"What are you? What do you call yourselves?" Katie asked.

"We are goblins, guardians of the magical world," Kittle said, quite matter-of-factly.

"But goblins don't exist!" Jacqui shouted. "Our dad taught us that in the Middle Ages, parents would tell their children stories of terrible goblins in the woods at night. This was to scare the children, so they wouldn't go outdoors at night and would stay away from the woods."

"Well," said Kittle, "you believe what you like, but you are looking at a goblin."

"Alright," said Katie, "you have a point. We now believe in goblins, so what are you doing following us?" As she spoke another four or five heads popped up out of the wheat field. They seemed to be just tall enough to look over the wheat, but only just. They all had the same facial features; big noses, ears and eyes, and bald heads.

"I've already told you," Kittle said. "We're guardians of the magical world."

"That doesn't explain why you're following us!" Adam shouted.

"We're following you, because you are on a magical journey to see Sofire."

"And who the hell is Sofire?" Adam responded.

"Don't talk about hell. Hell is a bad place. Hell is where devils come from. We are from the magical world, but we are not devils. Sofire has nothing to do with hell and nor do we!" Kittle shouted back and then vanished into the field of wheat.

"I think you said the wrong thing Adam. It's not your fault though. We are all in a new, stressful situation," said Katie. Who then shouted out at the top of her lungs, "We are sorry! We didn't mean to be rude! Please be our friends! We need help with this magical journey!" But nothing happened. They got no response, so they decided to continue their walk to the bridge.

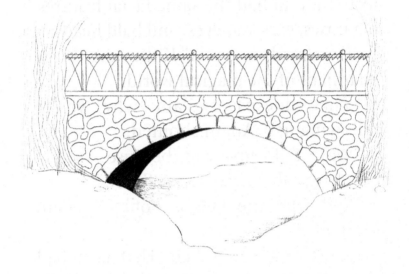

The Stone Bridge

Only then, as they walked, did Katie suddenly remember her mum's camera in her pocket. *No-one is ever going to believe us when we tell them what happened*, Katie thought. *Not unless I remember to take some pictures.*

"We still don't know what Sofire is. We're on a journey to find it and we don't know what it is," Katie said. "From what the goblin said, it's an animal or some sort of creature."

"It could be anything," Jacqui said, "but I bet it's a dragon."

"That's crazy," said Katie.

"Said by someone who has just been talking to goblins," Jacqui laughed.

"I think it's a heffalump," said Adam. "Everyone knows dragons don't exist, but I read a book called *Winnie-the-Pooh* and it talked about heffalumps. If it's in a book, it must be true."

"Yeah, right, of course. Why didn't I think of that?" replied Jacqui.

"We must try and learn as we go," said Katie. "We mustn't use the word hell for a start. That obviously upsets these creatures. And keep an eye out for heffalumps!" And she giggled as she said it.

Then as they walked on towards the stone bridge, a green, single-decker bus came from the left and slowed down as it drove carefully over the narrow bridge. A few yards further on it stopped at the side of the road. As the bus pulled away, an old lady appeared from behind it and she started making her way towards the bridge. She was moving slowly, so the children reached the bridge at the same time as her.

Katie suddenly had a thought and approaching the old lady said, "Excuse me madam, can I ask you a question?" As the old lady looked up at Katie, Katie had the weirdest feeling of knowing her.

"Yes, of course you can. What is it you want to know?"

"The route of that bus madam, does it go to the village Cwmtyr?"

"Certainly. Three stops further on, it stops outside the village shop. Then it turns left at the junction and goes into the main village," the old lady said.

"Wow," replied Katie, "that's perfect and where has the bus come from?"

"I don't know its full route," she replied. "The road, and hence the bus, follows the downstream course of the river Tyr, to this bridge. It then goes its own way to the village. I get on and off about a further mile upstream, near my daughter's cottage, by the mountain. That's all I know. I must walk on now. I am very tired today."

"We are sorry to delay you," Katie said, "but thank you very much. You have been very helpful. Diolch." As Katie said that, the old lady looked up at her and smiled, but a shiver ran down Katie's spine. Katie nearly collapsed but quickly recovered.

As Katie watched the old lady walk away, she suddenly realised the old lady's feet didn't seem to quite reach the ground. As crazy as that sounds, although the old lady appeared to walk, she actually glided along a couple of inches above the ground. Then Katie remembered her mum's camera, pulled it out of her pocket and took a photo of the old lady walking away. She checked she had the photo and then raised the camera to take more, but this time couldn't find the old lady in the viewfinder and, lowering the camera, could not see her anywhere. The old lady was nowhere to be seen, she had totally vanished. Katie turned to see if Jacqui or Adam had seen what had happened, but they were both feverishly searching the bridge for clues.

"Hey guys, did you see that old lady?" Katie said. "It was really strange, she gave me the heebie-jeebies. I nearly collapsed."

"Sorry, I didn't really take any notice of her," Jacqui said.

"After meeting those goblins, you now get frightened by an old lady," laughed Adam. "You're unreal Sis."

"It's a pity you two didn't speak to her," said Katie, "you would have understood then. She was really scary. She didn't walk away; she glided a couple of inches above the ground. She then just disappeared and why did she walk in the direction she had just come from, back towards her daughter's, instead of staying on the bus to the village? I think she got off the bus just to talk to us, if of course she really did get off the bus! You know that expression, your blood turning to ice? Well, now I know what it feels like."

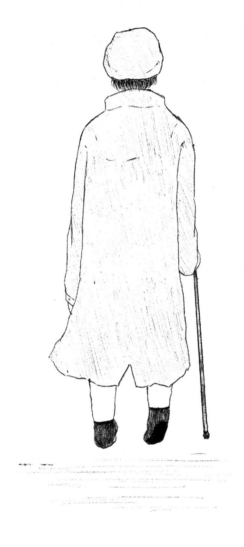

The old lady's feet didn't seem to quite reach the ground

Chapter 11
THE ADVENTURE CONTINUES

"I hate to interrupt the family chat, but can we get on please?" Jacqui moaned. "We need to find a stone, which is on or in the bridge and directly above the river. I guess it will be right in the centre of the bridge."

"It could be a loose stone, like the bricks in the loft," Adam suggested. They split up, Jacqui and Adam took one side of the bridge and Katie took the upstream side.

After a while Katie called out, "I think I may have found it." The others rushed over to Katie, who was hanging over the middle of the bridge. "I think there is writing on that stone down there, right in the middle. Trouble is it's the stone nearest the water. How are we going to read that clue?"

"I can think of a way, but Adam may

not like it," Jacqui said. "Katie, give Adam Mum's camera and show him how to work it. Then we hang Adam upside down over the side of the bridge, whilst he points the camera at the stone and presses the button."

"What do you think Adam?" Katie asked.

Adam thought about it, but wasn't very keen. He was usually prepared to take risks and sometimes without thinking, but on this occasion, the thought of being dropped into water put him off the idea. However, neither he nor his sisters could think of any other way they were going to get this clue.

"Adam, I promised Mum I would look after you," Katie said, "so I wouldn't let you do this, if I wasn't sure we could keep you safe. You are quite light, so Jacqui and I will be able to hold you safely. Jacqui will hang on to your right leg, while I'll hold your left leg and grip your belt with my right hand. You'll be fine."

"Okay," said Adam. "I just don't want to be dropped into the water; it's a long walk back sopping wet."

After Katie showed Adam how to use the camera, there were lots of dire threats from the girls, as to what would happen to him if he dropped Mum's camera in the river. This was followed by more threats, this time from Adam, as to what would happen to them, if they dropped him into the water!

Adam hung over the side of the bridge and the girls held his legs tightly, while Katie got a good grip on his belt, so his outstretched arms and camera were opposite the stone. There were a lot more threats from Adam, as to what he would do if they dropped him, but they didn't. The first three attempts at the photo, however, failed. Each time, the photo was out of focus or blurry, but the fourth attempt was a great success and the clue could be clearly read.

Katie had taken the camera back off Adam after the fourth attempt and was very pleased to see a clear picture of the side of the stone. She read aloud;

"Follow the Tyr and the water's course,
Up at the top you'll find its source,
Into the dark and deep in the cave,
To ask the question you'll have to be brave."

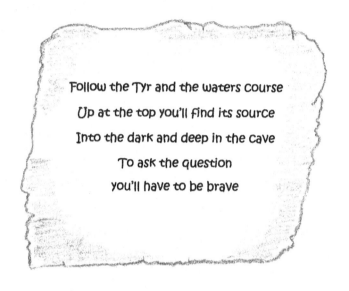

Follow the Tyr and the waters course
Up at the top you'll find its source
Into the dark and deep in the cave
To ask the question
you'll have to be brave

The Clue they found on the bridge

"That's amazing," said Jacqui, "that's carved into the stone. I can't see how that was done, unless it was carved into the stone before the bridge was built and this is a very old bridge."

"I've got a suggestion guys," said Katie. "We are going to run out of time if we're not careful." This was accompanied with a groan from Adam. "We have the clue, so I suggest we walk along to the bus stop and eat our packed lunches while we wait for a bus. We then get off at the village shop, as we know it's not a long walk back home from there."

"Actually, I think that's a great idea," said Jacqui.

After about half an hour, just when they had finished their packed lunches, the bus came. As they got off the bus, Jacqui asked the driver how frequently the bus came. Every hour he said, except Sunday, when there were only two buses all day. Jacqui thanked him and was about to get off the bus when a thought struck her.

"You must know this area fairly well," Jacqui said, "can I ask you a question?"

"Yes, go ahead," he said.

"We've been told the river Tyr comes from a cave. Do you know where that cave is? We'd love to explore," Jacqui said.

"You need to talk to the other driver. He's lived here all his life and knows everybody and everything around these parts. I'm quite new here. I can tell you the river starts in the mountains, a couple of miles up that road," he said pointing back the way they had just come. "They are not much more than hills, but last winter when the trees were bare, you got a clear view of them from here. You could see the snow on their peaks. It was a magnificent sight. I don't know about any cave though," the bus driver said.

Jacqui thanked the bus driver for his help and as the children walked to the door of the shop, Katie said, "That ties up with what the old lady said to me. She said her daughter's cottage is next to the mountain, which is about a mile up the road from the bridge. That would be about two miles from here. If the source of the river is that mountain, that must be where the cave is."

"That makes sense. Tomorrow we should get the bus all the way up to the mountain and have a look," said Jacqui, as the three of them went into the village shop. Adam was after some chocolate and was hoping their meagre resources would stretch to a bar or two.

The children all said good day in Welsh (with an English accent of course) and it made the shopkeeper smile. Adam managed to get enough money from Katie for two bars of chocolate, so he happily shared them with the others. The shop was otherwise empty and Katie got chatting with the owner. Katie was obviously not telling her about their adventure, if any of them did that they would all get carted away for treatment at the nearest mental health hospital, but she did mention the old lady on the bridge. The shopkeeper couldn't think who that might have been, which was unusual, as she thought she knew everyone who lived in and around the village. Then Katie remembered she had a picture of the old lady on her mum's camera.

"It's only a photo from the rear," Katie said, "she was walking away at the time." Katie found the picture and brought it on to full screen and turned the camera around so the shopkeeper could see it. The shopkeeper stepped forward and leant over to get a good look and as she did so, she went totally white. All the blood seemed to drain from her face and she had to grab the shop counter to stop herself from falling over.

"Oh, my God," she said and kept saying it, over and over again. Katie, Jacqui and Adam had no idea what the problem was and no idea what to do. Then Jacqui spotted a chair and pulled it over and they sat the shopkeeper down.

"Here," said Katie, "before you fall down."

"Thank you," she said. "I've had a bit of a shock. I know that lady in your picture. I know the photo is from behind, but I easily recognise her. That's the hat and coat she always wore."

"Well," said Jacqui, "who is it?"

"It's definitely Mrs Carruthers," the shopkeeper said, with a tremor in her voice.

Katie thought she recognised that name and then it struck her. She remembered her mum mentioning the name 'Carruthers' when she was signing the legal documents, back in Hastings, to buy the cottage. This very old lady couldn't be the daughter, so that didn't leave many other possibilities!

Now, Katie was feeling like she needed to sit down. Katie realised she was holding the shop counter so tightly her hands were turning white. Of course, now some things began to make sense. Katie had shivered when the old lady looked at her and when the old lady walked away, she didn't seem to be walking; it was more like gliding over the ground. The old lady had talked about her visits to her daughter, who did in fact live a further mile up the road from the bridge. Katie had assumed she had just come from her daughter's cottage.

"That was a ghost, wasn't it?" Katie said. "The ghost of the previous owner of our cottage?"

The shopkeeper was in shock and couldn't bring herself to admit it. She could only nod her head. Then after a while she said, "I don't know if it has any relevance, but everyone in the village believed she was a witch. I always thought she was a good witch. She seemed to help people, not hurt them. But seeing your photo today has been a shock for me. I will close my shop and go up for a lie down." She reached out and took another bar of chocolate and gave it to Adam. "That's for free dearie. It's on the house, as they say." And she walked unsteadily towards the shop front door and turned over the sign to say closed. The children thanked her, wished her well and left the shop.

Chapter 12
'SPARKIE'

The children walked away from the shop. At first, they weren't saying anything. Each one was caught up with their own thoughts.

After a while Katie said, "We have had strange things happen, we've met real live goblins and now I've actually seen and talked with a ghost. Do either of you want to call a halt to this adventure?"

Jacqui and Adam looked at each other and both shook their heads and together said, "No way!"

"Good," said Katie. "The weird happenings and the strange creatures all seem to be helping us. I still don't think we are in danger. We move on then." Together they turned and started walking towards the cottage.

"Maybe if Mrs Carruthers was a witch," said Jacqui, "she was a friend of the goblins.

Think about it. This has all started since we moved into the cottage. The first clue was at the cottage. The cottage itself tried to tell us, with the weird noise and orange light. And along the journey the goblins have been following us, but never trying to stop us. Maybe Mrs Carruthers asked the goblins to help us."

Then Adam grabbed Jacqui's arm. "Have you realised a cat is following us?" Adam asked.

Jacqui and Katie stopped walking and turned around to find a young, ginger cat walking in circles. It was obvious it was waiting for them to walk on. Katie smiled and Jacqui shrugged her shoulders and they pretended to ignore it.

When they arrived back at 'Minafon' the cat was still with them and when they opened the front door, the cat immediately rushed inside as though it was coming home. Their mum was due back from work in an hour, so Katie decided to ring Jenny at the care home. When Jenny came to the phone, Katie could tell she was panicky and

Katie had to reassure her mum all was well.

"No Mum, everything is fine. It's just that a cat seems to have taken a liking to us and has come in the house like she owns it. We don't know anything about the cat. It could be a stray, but it's acting like it is here to stay. Can you get some cat food on the way back from work please? By the way, the corner shop is closed, so I don't know; maybe the petrol station will do cat food. No Mum, no problems. We are fine, just hungry. Come home safe."

That's weird, Katie thought. *All this crazy stuff going on and I'm telling Mum to be safe.*

Katie went to the back door and hung the back door key on its hook. Then she went to the fridge to see what there was for tea and spotted the two cooked sausages left over from the sausage and mash on Sunday night. She took one out and chopped it up. She then went searching for the cat and found it happily curled up, asleep on Jacqui's bed.

Sparkie, making herself at home on Jacqui's bed

It looks like, it's decided to stay, she thought, as she left the plate of chopped sausage on the floor next to the bed.

Jenny was totally shattered when she got back from work and told the children she hadn't been able to get any cat food.

"It's okay Mum," said Katie, "I gave the cat some chopped up sausage. We can get some cat food tomorrow if you leave some money out for us."

Jenny hardly had the strength to make the children scrambled eggs on toast. She then opened tins of rice pudding and tins of ready-made custard to fill their tummies. She found the bowl they'd used to feed the cat and it was empty, so Jenny put water in it. They all went to bed and Jenny noticed how quiet it was now; not even the noise from the loft. She wondered about that, but not for long, as she quickly fell asleep.

She was in a deep sleep, when she was suddenly woken by a horrible screech! She jumped out of bed and nearly stepped on the cat. Jenny quickly realised it had been the cat that had made that loud screeching noise. The cat was stretching up to its maximum height, its ears were flat and it was hissing at something. Jenny couldn't actually see what was causing the cat to hiss, but the cat had definitely found something it didn't like. Jenny grabbed the cat and put it outside her bedroom door, vowing to make sure her door was closed in future. As she put the cat down, Katie and Jacqui appeared, wondering what all the noise was about.

Adam must be in a deep sleep, Jenny thought, *as his bedroom is next to mine and all this noise hasn't disturbed him.*

Jacqui noticed the cat was agitated and still hissing and said the cat was 'sparking off', as she called it. Katie immediately decided to name her Sparkie.

"You can call it what you like guys, but keep her out of my bedroom. I need to sleep," Jenny said and went back to bed. As Jenny lay down to sleep she suddenly had a horrible thought. *The old lady, Mrs Carruthers, died in this room and she was supposed to be a witch. Don't they say that cats can sense ghosts? No, that's crazy*, she thought, *I'm just trying to scare myself.* She turned over and thankfully, in a matter of minutes, was asleep again.

Katie and Jacqui went back to bed and agreed they would get up early, so they could all be ready to leave immediately after Mum left for work. Happy with their plan, they turned out the light and quickly fell asleep. The cottage stayed peaceful for the rest of the night and they all slept well.

Chapter 13
JOURNEY TO THE CAVE

Katie awoke and could hear Mum moving around, so she quietly climbed out of bed and went over to Jacqui. She gently shook her and whispered to her to wake up and get washed and dressed.

"Don't show any excitement Jacqui," Katie whispered, "or Mum will realise something is up." Katie then went to wake up Adam, but found he was already up and dressed. She also warned Adam not to show any enthusiasm.

"You are normally slow and half asleep when you get up Adam. If you bounce around the house with a smile on your face, Mum will know we are up to something. Be quiet and a bit miserable. Okay?"

"Yeah, no problem," said Adam.

"Good. Go down and have some breakfast. It could be a long day."

After breakfast, Katie told Jenny they were going to walk to the village shop and get some cat food.

"Can we have some money for it and also some pocket money please? We'd like to buy sweets and maybe a magazine."

"Look Katie," Jenny said, "we might not have a mortgage to pay now but I don't get paid until next week, so I have to be very careful. I do have a little money left from the sale of our old house, but it has to last until I get paid. That's all I can spare for now, so you'll have to make it last." Jenny gave Katie a few coins and after kissing them all, she rushed off to work.

Jenny had the strangest feeling that she was 'missing something' but couldn't put her finger on it. The children seemed happier than they had been for a very long time. She believed they were old enough and sensible enough to stay safe, so she was going to try not to worry about them. Tomorrow was Friday and she was not working Friday to Sunday, so she would plan to spend time with the children;

something to look forward to.

Katie organised Jacqui and Adam into making their packed lunches, whilst she got some drink bottles, her mum's camera and the torch for the backpacks. They locked the front door, put the key in the secret hiding place and marched off to the village. The village shop was open, so they went in and bought a chocolate bar. They hoped they would remember to get the cat food on the way back, as they didn't want to carry it all day. The shopkeeper seemed to have recovered from her fright the day before. She didn't mention anything about the 'ghost', so Katie thought it best not to raise the subject.

"We thought we would go for a bus ride today, to explore the area," Katie said. "Go and see the mountain. Do you know what time the bus will be here?"

The shopkeeper looked sternly at them and said, "The bus will be here in ten minutes or so. You are not going to walk up the mountain are you? It's very dangerous up there; lots of pebbles and rocks. It would be very easy to twist an ankle or fall."

"No, don't worry. We are only going for a look-see," Katie replied. The shopkeeper nodded and the children left the shop.

As predicted, the bus arrived in about ten minutes and they climbed on board. The driver was an elderly, unshaven man with grey hair. He wore spectacles with very thick lenses, which made his eyes look very large, but he had a lovely smile and seemed friendly.

"We have been told about a mountain, about two miles up the road from here," Katie said to the driver. "We hear it might have a cave and we thought it would be fun to see it. Do you know where it is?"

The smile on the driver's face had immediately vanished as he said, "Listen children. I know where this cave is, but many people in the village believe that a monster lives in the cave. There are stories of people who have gone into the cave and never been seen again. I'm sure it's all a load of rubbish, but I think it's best you don't go inside the cave."

"We won't," Jacqui said. "We just want to see it. We won't go inside, we promise."

"Okay," the bus driver said. He told them how much the tickets were and after they paid, he said he would tell them where to get off the bus.

The children sat at the back of the bus and Jacqui whispered to the others, "I must admit, I hate all this lying. We haven't actually lied to Mum but we aren't telling her the truth either."

Katie leant across and said, "I know, but we are lying to the shopkeeper and the bus driver. Look Jacqui, you know as well as I do, if we tell anyone the truth, they will immediately stop us."

Adam listened to this and whispered, "When we find out about the treasure, can we tell Mum immediately? I don't like not telling Mum and I want her to be part of this."

The two girls nodded their agreement.

Adam, the youngest

The bus travelled very slowly along the narrow, twisty country lane and had to stop twice to let a car come past from the opposite direction.

The road began to climb upwards and after another few minutes the bus stopped and the driver turned around in his seat and said, "This is your stop children." He pointed over to the right and said, "There is a mountain stream on the right over there, which is the beginning of the river Tyr. It flows from a cave about halfway up the mountain. Just follow the stream and you'll find the cave. It's a good 20-minute climb though. You will have to be very careful. Do your parents know you are doing this?"

"Yes sir," said Katie as they climbed off the bus, "our mum knows and she trusts us to be sensible."

"Then make sure you are. The bus comes back this way every hour, so I'll look out for you later," he said, and with that, drove off.

The children crossed the narrow lane and found the stream on the other side. The two girls adjusted their backpacks on their backs and the three of them started the upward climb. The ground was very uneven and there were loose stones underfoot and large rocks that they had to go around. The thistles and gorse bushes added to their problems, but they pressed on and up. So much for the 20-minute climb, it was closer to an hour by the time they were standing in front of the entrance to the cave.

Chapter 14
LIFE OR DEATH?

The children were hot, sweaty and breathless by then. Jacqui was thinking to herself how unfit she was, whilst Katie was blaming the weight of the backpack. Nevertheless, they had at last found the cave. They were fairly sure this entire magical adventure was all about what was in this cave. On the left-hand side of the entrance to the cave, was where the stream flowed out, trickling over small stones in a gully. This was the beginning of the river Tyr. Keeping to the right of the cave, they nervously walked inside into the gloom. There was no lighting, but the entrance of the cave was just light enough to see. Katie found herself feeling nervous and also guilty, as they had made a promise to the bus driver not to enter the cave.

As they slowly walked further into the

cave a large shadow in the corner moved. They froze. *That is no shadow, it definitely moved*, thought Katie.

"Stand still guys," Katie said, as she pulled out her mum's torch from her backpack, "I think we have company." As she shone the torch towards the dark corner of the cave, the 'shadow' rose up and started walking towards them. It was very large. Its head nearly touched the roof of the cave, which was at least ten feet above the floor. Its head however, was actually small for its size, while its stomach, arms and legs were huge. But what the three children couldn't take their eyes off was the largest fighting club they could ever imagine, which it held in its right hand.

It opened its mouth and showed a row of yellow, broken teeth. When it spoke to them, it sounded like gravel in a cement mixer.

"Do not point that torch at my face. Point it at the ground. But you do not need to be afraid, we have been expecting you. I am the guardian of the cave. No-one comes in here without my say-so. But you

Gothic, a huge Mountain Troll

are welcome and can come in."

"You must be the reason for all the stories in the village of a monster in the cave. What is your name? What are you?" asked Jacqui, a tremble in her voice.

"They call me Gothic, I am a mountain troll. I live in the cave."

"Why do you carry that huge club?" Adam asked, pointing nervously to the massive fighting club.

"That is to frighten off anyone who is not welcome. But as I said, you are welcome, so do not worry."

Adam couldn't imagine that Gothic needed the club. *Everyone would still be afraid of him without any club*, he thought.

Gothic stepped to one side and waved the three of them further into the cave.

"Keep to the right, away from the stream," said Gothic, "and keep your torch pointed at the ground ahead of you. At the end of the tunnel there is better lighting. There is also a swirling pool of water on the left. You must not enter or touch that pool. The water is pure. It is the source of the river, but it is also the drinking water for those of us who live here, including Sofire. After you pass the pool of water on your left, you will meet Joker around the next bend."

When Gothic turned around and walked back to his corner, they felt the tremor in the ground from his footfalls! Then Katie remembered she should take photos, otherwise no-one would believe them, and pulled out her mum's camera. Jacqui saw her and immediately grabbed her hand.

"Turn off the flash Katie; you saw how he hated the torch. Ask if he minds you taking a photo, don't just do it. You really don't want this chap angry."

Katie nodded and called out, "Excuse me Gothic, do you mind if I take your photo?"

Gothic immediately turned back and raised his club and shouted so loud, they thought the walls of the cave trembled.

"You cannot take any photos at all, of this cave or in this cave! We hide in here from humans and just one photo would make us a tourist attraction! You do not take photos and be careful who you tell!"

"We understand," said Katie and with nervous looks over their shoulders they started down the tunnel, keeping to the right-hand side.

The tunnel was carved out of solid rock and was about 10-foot high and 12-foot across. As they walked down the tunnel it got darker, but Katie kept the torch pointed at the ground to light their way. They could also see that at the end of the tunnel the lighting improved. When they got there, they found that the tunnel opened out into another cavern and several flaming torches were fixed to the walls. On their left was the pool of bright swirling water, which fed the stream. The centre of the pool bubbled and frothed. The flames of the torches reflected on the moving water creating a kaleidoscope of colour and beauty; a truly magical cavern.

"We were told about these at school," Jacqui said. "That is a natural spring. The water comes from an aquifer, which is probably deep in the mountain. The water may be hot or cold, but this one's probably cold because there's no steam coming off it."

Adam stepped forward and bent over with an outstretched hand, but Katie immediately grabbed his arm.

"I was only going to put my hand in to find out," Adam said.

"That's exactly what Gothic said you mustn't do. Your hands will be filthy and this is their drinking water," Katie said.

"I see. I didn't think. You're right Sis."

Adam stood up and the three of them walked past the pool. A little further on they found Joker, who turned out to be another goblin and was waiting to greet them. He was also no taller than Adam, had big eyes, nose and ears, a bald head and his hands and feet were claws. Like Noogan, the goblin in the woods, he held a staff. From Joker's expression and demeanour, it was obvious to Jacqui that the other goblins were probably being sarcastic when they gave him the name of Joker. He looked very serious. Jacqui had never seen anyone less likely to crack jokes. Nevertheless, he seemed to be friendly.

Joker, a serious Goblin

"Welcome to our humble home," he said. "I hope you are ready to face the challenge. To win the right to meet Sofire, you must ask a question. Only one of you can ask the question and you do not have a second chance if you get it wrong. From this cavern, there are two further tunnels and at the entrance of each tunnel there is another goblin. One goblin always tells the truth and the other goblin always lies. The problem is that you do not know which is which. You can only ask one question to one of the goblins and you need to find out which tunnel you must go down to meet Sofire."

"If we choose the correct tunnel," Katie said, "we get to meet Sofire, but if we go down the wrong tunnel, what happens?"

"We call it life or death," Joker said. "If you choose the correct tunnel, you will have the adventure of your life. If you choose the wrong tunnel, you will all wake up in bed and this adventure will have died. You will not remember anything that has happened to you. The magical world will die in you. That will be due to 'Tinsel', who you may meet if you are successful."

"Can you help us with the question?" asked Adam.

"I can tell you about yourselves, but I cannot help you with the question," said Joker.

"Please tell us what you can," said Katie. Joker looked at the three of them, with a very serious expression.

"You remind me of the friends on the

yellow brick road. You each have several weaknesses, but each of you also has one strength. Adam, you are the brave warrior. Katie, you are the organiser and leader, but Jacqui, you are the intellect, the tactician. You, Jacqui, must ask the question. You can take as long as you want, but can only ask one goblin once."

Jacqui turned to the other two. "If I am to answer this riddle I need total silence and to be left alone until I have solved it. If I can't solve it, if they allow us, we will have to go home. We must not ask the wrong question. Are we in agreement?"

Katie and then Adam nodded and Jacqui went off into the corner of the cavern and found a flat rock she could sit on, while she pondered. She put her head in her hands and the others waited in silence. The minutes ticked by and after an hour Katie was about to tell Jacqui they must go home and think about it there, when Jacqui suddenly stood up and went over to Joker.

"Where are the goblins I must speak to?" Jacqui asked. Joker pointed at the two tunnel entrances. Jacqui went to one of the tunnels and found one of the goblins.

"If you asked your goblin friend over there," she said as she pointed to the other entrance, "which tunnel would lead to Sofire, which tunnel would your goblin friend say?"

The goblin thought about it and then pointed at his own tunnel. Jacqui smiled and went over to Katie and Adam and said they had to use the other tunnel.

"But are you sure, Jacqui?" Katie said.

"Yes, I'm sure," she said and walked over to the other tunnel. As they walked past the other goblin, he smiled at them and clapped his hands. Jacqui smiled back and they walked on.

"I don't understand how you worked that out Jacqui," Adam said.

"Think about it, Adam. One goblin only lies and one goblin only tells the truth. I asked one goblin to ask the other goblin, which is the correct tunnel. If the goblin I am speaking to tells the truth, his friend will lie and he will tell me the wrong tunnel. If I am speaking to the goblin that lies, his friend will tell the truth, but the goblin I asked will lie to me and say the other tunnel. Either way, I will be told the wrong tunnel, so we have gone down the other tunnel."

"Wow, that's really clever Jacqui. By getting one goblin to ask the other goblin, either way you will get a lie and know to do the opposite."

"Yes, that's it exactly," Jacqui said pride evident in her voice. As they spoke they walked around a corner in the tunnel and found themselves looking at a massive cavern with a huge domed roof.

Chapter 15
'SOFIRE'

Katie, Jacqui and Adam stepped inside the cavern and totally froze. In front of them was what looked like a huge dragon! At first Katie thought it must be an elaborate carving, or maybe it was dead, but then she realised she could see the rise and fall of its sides. It was breathing! Then one huge eye suddenly opened and all three of the children involuntarily jumped backwards. Then the other eye opened. Its eyes were crimson with irises like a snake's, but a hundred times bigger. Just the eyes were enough to scare anyone to death!

Even lying down, the dragon was the size of a single-decker bus. Its skin was scaly and bright green! They could see huge claws that protruded from its front feet that were like talons. Like the feet of an eagle, but many times bigger. They could now hear its breathing. It sounded laboured, as though it wasn't well.

It was now awake and lifted its head. Its massive mouth opened, showing large, pointed teeth with gaps in between. The three children screamed and jumped back.

'Sofire, awakes to greet the children'

"Oh, I'm sorry," it said, in a very deep voice that echoed around the cavern. "I only needed to yawn."

"You can speak!" Adam cried out.

"Of course, I can. I have had many, many years to learn many things," Sofire replied.

"I am sorry," Adam said. "The other magical creatures all talk. For some strange reason, I didn't think a dragon would talk."

"Are you Sofire, the one the goblins have talked about?" Katie asked.

"That's right," the dragon replied.

"Now I understand your name, So Fire!" Katie replied. "I would have guessed, except I didn't believe in dragons. Do you really breathe fire then?"

"I used to be able to, but not now, I'm too old. I am now the only living dragon. Fire breathing is not about self-protection, it's about awakening the eggs."

"How old are you?" Adam asked.

"That's not a question you should ask a lady, Adam," said the dragon.

"How do you know my name?" Adam replied.

"Your family bought an old cottage from a lady who also has magical powers," Sofire said. "She wanted you to have her cottage. She talks to the goblins. The goblins talk to me. So, there is very little I don't know Adam, except maybe my age. In answer to your question, I'm not totally sure, but I guess about a thousand years old."

The children gasped at that.

"That doesn't make sense, Sofire," Jacqui said. "You are telling us dragons live for a thousand years and you are huge and powerful. So how is it you are the only dragon who has survived? What has happened to the other dragons?"

"When I was young," Sofire said, "all the countries were ruled by kings. When a king was approaching the end of his life, the young princes would all compete to take over the crown and be the new king. However, the only thing that would totally convince the people that a prince was courageous enough to be the new king would be if the prince killed a dragon. Some princes were fair and did try to kill a dragon with only a sword and shield, but many were not so brave and would get their men to use a cannon and then claim the victory, waving their sword. Slowly there were less and less of us and so we hid from the world in dark caves like this."

The three children stood and sadly thought about what they had just been told.

"So, when you die, Sofire," Katie said, "there will never be another dragon!"

"That would be true, except my parents laid four eggs and only hatched one, me. I have kept the other three eggs and will entrust them to people who will hatch them, when they can safely protect my brothers and sisters."

"Who will these people be?" Adam asked.

"They have to prove themselves," said Sofire. "I asked the goblins to help me and they devised three quests, which have clues and a difficult question. Those who make it to my cave have earned the right to care for one of the eggs."

"That means us!" shouted Adam and jumped up and down.

"It does, Adam, but it's a huge responsibility. You need to think about it first."

"Wait a minute," Katie said. "If these dragon eggs are your brothers and sisters, they must also be a thousand years old. Eggs don't last a thousand years. Don't they have to be kept warm and then they hatch immediately?"

Sofire threw back her head and laughed, but the action and noise seriously scared the children!

"Sorry, I didn't mean to frighten you. Katie, you are thinking of chicken eggs. These are dragon eggs. Dragon eggs last forever and have to be hatched by a dragon breathing fire on it. If a dragon is not available, then putting the egg in a real flame fire will hatch it."

"Won't it cook the egg instead?" Katie asked.

"No. Dragons are magic and so are their eggs, so normal rules don't apply to us. How do you think we fly? Look at the size of me. In your world, my wings would have to be absolutely enormous. Magic helps me fly, magic gives me a thousand years and magic makes our eggs hatch."

"I still don't understand how we are to help," Jacqui said. "We do not know anything about dragons, so we are not able to care for a dragon egg, let alone a baby dragon. We don't know how to feed it or care for it."

"If you agree to help, you will be the guardian of one egg and then, of course, a baby dragon. The egg, and then the baby dragon, will stay here with me, in this cave, as I will have to raise it and teach it everything it needs to know. But you guys will name it and visit it regularly, and if I should die, or be killed, before the baby is grown and able to fend for itself, you will have to do your best to protect it. As far as the young dragon is concerned, Gothic and all the goblins will help and serve you. There is also one very important magical creature you have yet to meet."

Sofire raised her head further and called with a deep rumbling sound, "Tinsel come to us!"

Sofire raises her head and calls Tinsel

Chapter 16
THE ELVEN QUEEN

There was immediately a sound, like a rushing wind, and a fog seemed to appear and began swirling around them. The children were at first frightened but quickly realised, as Sofire was relaxed and waiting, there wasn't anything to worry about. The noise of the wind stopped and as the fog cleared, they found they were looking at a beautiful, young lady. She had fair skin, long blonde hair and a very pretty face. She wore a tight-fitting, one-piece bodice, together with a circular black pendant hanging from her neck, black, thigh-length boots and similar material on both arms. The children could see that her ears were long and pointed, like the goblins, but they weren't grotesque. In fact, they seemed to add to her beauty.

"I would like you to meet Tinsel," Sofire

said, as the beautiful lady raised her hand in welcome. "Tinsel is an elven queen and must therefore be shown respect. Do not be misguided by her beauty, she has magical powers and will help you to protect your dragon when I am no longer around."

"How can she help us?" asked Adam.

"As I said, Tinsel is magical. She can appear and disappear at will, but has one amazing power. She can read minds, anyone's mind. More than that, she can wipe memories from their minds as well," Sofire replied.

"That was what Joker was talking about, wasn't it?" said Adam.

"Yes," said Sofire. "How do you think a dragon like me has lived here for one thousand years and nobody has ever discovered me and told the world? Well, there have been those who have met the goblins, or Gothic, or wandered into my cave and some who have even found me. It has happened many times in a thousand years, but Tinsel takes away their memory. It doesn't hurt them, but they wake up the

Tinsel, The Elven Queen

next day and just can't remember what they did the day before. Have you never woken up and couldn't remember what you did the day before?"

"Yes, I guess so," said Jacqui. "But I don't really understand. Tinsel, you are very young and Sofire says you have been protecting her for all this time."

Sofire, however, answered. "Yes, that's right. That's the magic. Tinsel doesn't age. She looks like she is a teenager, but is even older than me. For over a thousand years everyone has heard of Tinsel. Something sparkling and magical, but people just don't know where the word comes from, or who she is."

"Wow," said Adam, "I just thought it was the name we gave to certain Christmas decorations."

And Tinsel smiled.

"Well, we are very pleased to meet you Tinsel," Jacqui said and bowed to her, followed by Katie and Adam, who also bowed. Jacqui continued, "I have been thinking about everything you have said

Sofire. I would ask two things. Firstly, we cannot do any of these things unless we tell our mother and she agrees. For us to regularly visit and take on this responsibility, our mum would need to know where we were and what we were doing. We have been lying to our mother by not telling her what we have been doing and we cannot, and do not want to, continue to lie to her. Our mum is not working tomorrow. Can we bring her here to meet you all and speak with you? If she agrees, then we can take responsibility. If she doesn't agree, I guess Tinsel, you will make us forget. Secondly, we need to leave now, to be back before our mum gets home, but can we see the eggs first, before we leave?"

Tinsel then spoke, "You are very welcome to bring your mother to meet us here tomorrow. We will tell Gothic to expect you all."

Sofire then said, "In answer to your second question…"

Sofire rose up on her rear legs and spread

her wings. The children were shocked by the sudden movement and the size of her, and leapt backwards, but then Adam and Katie both said "Wow" together, as they saw the three large dragon eggs that had been concealed under her wings.

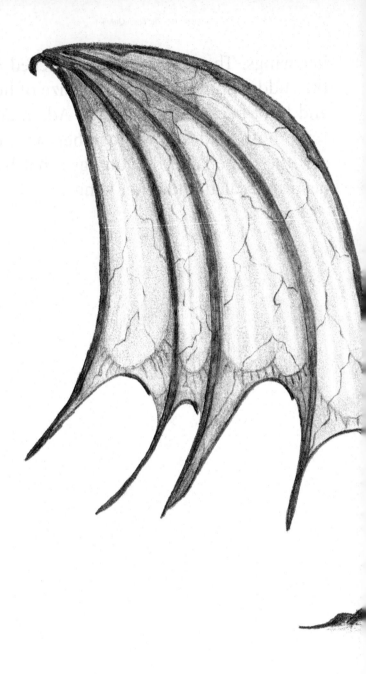

Sofire reveals the eggs...

When the children climbed back on the bus, the driver said how pleased he was to see them safe and sound. However, they didn't tell the driver they had ignored their promise to him and gone into the cave. They got off the bus at the village shop and then walked home with hardly a word said between them. Each one was deep in thought. It was impossible to take in what they had seen and done in the last four days. Somehow, they had to persuade their mother to let them go along with this crazy adventure.

The responsibility and problems had yet to even start. It would affect all the family and probably for their entire lives! The alternative was that Tinsel would wipe away their memories and they would return to a normal life, living in an old cottage in Wales. Not a disaster, they were happy and loved each other, but how many get the opportunity to see the magical world that most people don't even believe in?

Jenny didn't even get through the door before all three children started telling her different accounts of goblins and dragons! Jenny could see there was some sort of crisis, so she told them to be quiet, as she made a cup of tea.

Then she took them into the lounge and gave each one in turn, a chance to talk. After about 20 minutes Jenny had some idea of the story. She didn't believe a word of it, but the children were all saying the same thing and were insistent that it was totally true. Jenny had been hoping to spend time with her children over the next three days and it might as well start off with a trip with them to this cave. Anyway, she had to get to the bottom of this crazy story. She'd take a picnic basket and hope the weather would be good.

Chapter 17
THE DREAM BECOMES REALITY

The next morning Jenny woke up as if having been in a dream. Then slowly she realised two things.

The first thing was that it wasn't a dream. Her supposedly sane children had last night been telling her about meeting magical creatures, such as goblins and dragons. Because all three of the children had been telling her the same story, she'd had agreed to go to this cave with them.

The second thing was that as it was Friday that day, she didn't have to go into work; something positive to hang on to. So, she got up, washed and dressed, and went downstairs to prepare breakfast for them all.

However, on arrival in the kitchen, she

found out that all three children were up and had been up for some time. Katie was in the kitchen and was making toast for herself.

"Look Katie," Jenny said, "whatever is going on, I need you to let me have breakfast in peace and then when I'm ready to listen, I want you to talk me through it, just the two of us for now." So, after breakfast Katie and Jenny sat at the kitchen table sipping their tea.

"Mum, I've been talking to Jacqui and Adam half the night and have been awake thinking for the rest of the night," said Katie. "We have already told you most of what happened and whatever else we say, you won't be able to believe it. We've seen it and we are still struggling to believe it. So, we are going to start from the beginning, but not tell you, but show you instead. You must trust us and go along with it. Don't ask questions, just watch and listen. You will know as much as us by the end of the day and then we can talk."

"Okay, I'm going to trust you and go

along with this," Jenny replied. "What happens next?"

"We have all had breakfast and been waiting for you Mum. I'll get the others. We are starting in the loft."

They took Jenny up into the loft, told her about the humming noise, which of course Jenny had already heard, then told her about the orange light and showed their mum the loose bricks and the little metal door with a key. They then brought Mum downstairs and showed her the scroll with the clue written on it. Jenny was really good and very patient. She just looked and listened, but didn't say a word.

They then asked Jenny to take them all for a drive. Jenny quickly prepared a picnic basket and then changed her shoes which had heels, for a pair of sensible walking shoes. Last night the children had been talking about a cave and she wanted to be prepared for anything. She collected her jacket and keys, and locked up the house. With a strange wry smile on her face and a shaking of her head, Jenny climbed into the car. Jacqui directed her mum to drive to the stone bridge where they parked the car on a nearby grass verge.

Katie explained how they'd worked out the first clue and followed the river to the bridge. She leant over the bridge and told her mum how they'd read the clue on the bridge. At that point, thinking of how dangerous that would have been for Adam, Jenny nearly lost her patience, but she had promised to go along with this, so she bit her tongue and stayed calm. As they walked back to the car, Katie told Jenny about their meetings with Noogan and Kittle. She said she didn't expect Jenny to believe her, but that was okay, because she would see for herself very soon.

When they got back in the car, Jacqui sat next to their mum and she asked Jenny to drive to the mountain. As before, they parked on a convenient grass verge and then they slowly climbed up the side of the mountain, following the stream. Jenny hadn't really noticed the weather, partly because it was non-problematic; mild, overcast and dry, mainly though, because her thoughts were totally overwhelmed by the children's stories and the fear of the unknown. Jenny did however notice the steep, uneven ground under their feet, with pebbles and loose pieces of rock, which made it a hazardous climb. She was very pleased she had taken the time to change her shoes before she had left the house. When they arrived outside the cave they all rested for a while, trying to get their breath back. Jacqui was the first to recover and reminded their mum of the stories they'd told her last night of the mountain troll.

"Well Mum, this is when you meet him," Adam said. "His name is Gothic. He is huge and scary, but he is okay as long as you don't take any photos. That makes him cross." As Adam said this, the three children started to walk into the entrance of the cave. Jenny was shaking her head and was beginning to believe that her children had been given drugs. She could not think of any other reason for these mad stories. Then as they walked into the cave, the large shadow in the corner of the cave moved. Gothic rose up and started walking towards them. Jenny screamed and wanted to run away, but she knew she couldn't leave her children alone with this monster.

"You must be their mum," Gothic said, his voice deep and gravelly like a cement mixer in a well.

Jenny hadn't realised she had grabbed the hands of Jacqui and Adam, until Adam cried out, "Mum, you are hurting us. You are squeezing our hands!" At which point Jenny realised and loosened her grip.

"Mum, it's okay. Gothic is here to guard the cave. He won't hurt us," Katie said.

Realising he was frightening Jenny, Gothic stepped back and told the family to go through and meet Joker. Jenny's face had gone pale and her eyes were wide.

"What or who is Joker?" Jenny asked.

"Oh, he's okay Mum. He's just a goblin. You'll like him. He's not even scary," said Adam, walking towards the tunnel.

Katie and Jacqui had each grabbed one of Mum's hands and walked with her behind

Adam, who seemed to be enjoying every minute of this.

They walked slowly down the tunnel, passed the colourful swirling pool and went around the corner where they met Joker.

In a way, Adam was right. After meeting Gothic, the goblins were a walk in the park. Nevertheless, by the time the family arrived in Sofire's cavern, Jenny's eyes had glazed over. She looked like she was in a dream, or should one say a nightmare. The family were standing in front of Sofire, but Jenny hadn't even reacted. Whether in the dim light she hadn't seen Sofire yet, or whether meeting a mountain troll, three goblins and a dragon in one morning was too much for her, wasn't clear.

Chapter 18
THE MAGICAL WORLD

Sofire's eyes slowly opened; well she was a thousand years old.

She raised her great head as she said, "Welcome Jenny to my home. Welcome to the magical world. Most people haven't even heard of it. Of the people who have heard of the magical world, most don't believe in it. Nevertheless, we have invited your family to become part of it. It is all about these eggs." As Sofire said this, she rose up on her rear legs, as she had done before, and lifted her wings to expose the three great dragon eggs.

Sofire continued. "Your children may have told you already, but I am now very old and the time has come to bring my brothers and sisters into this world. With the help of the goblins, I have devised three quests for the three eggs. Your children have passed one of these quests and we have asked them to consider becoming a guardian for one of the young dragons. I would like you to meet Tinsel, who is an elven queen, and who will still be around even when I have gone."

As Sofire mentioned Tinsel's name, there was again the sound of a rushing wind and a mist appeared in front of Sofire. Katie and Jacqui, knowing what was coming, stood even closer to their mother and gripped her hands tightly. Adam was beaming with delight and very nearly jumping up and down. As promised, Jenny had hardly said a word all morning and continued to be in a dreamlike state. She had seen so much in such a short time. If Peter Pan himself had flown in, Jenny would have casually greeted him.

When the rushing wind slowed down and stopped, and the mist evaporated, Tinsel could be clearly seen, her beauty and poise radiating across the cavern.

"My name is Tinsel," she said to Jenny. "I am an elven queen. I am very pleased to meet you Jenny. This must be very hard for you. Your children have been introduced to this magical world through a series of revelations over the last four days. You on the other hand, have met a mountain troll, three goblins, a dragon and now myself, in the course of one morning." As Tinsel said this, Jenny smiled and nodded.

That being said, Jenny had coped extremely well, and had taken in and understood everything that had happened around her.

Tinsel then spoke at length to Jenny and explained the serious responsibilities the children would be taking on, if the Jackson family agreed to adopt one of the dragon eggs. Tinsel then went on to further explain that if the family did take on this responsibility, the relationship between this magical world and the Jackson family would become a two-way arrangement. In other words, the magical world, including the goblins, trolls, elves, fairies and herself, would always be there, even after Sofire was not around. They would all respond, support and protect the Jackson family. The family would never have to worry about money for food, clothing or bills. Magic would ensure their needs would always be met.

After two long years of struggling to pay the bills and not having enough money to properly feed her children, Jenny felt that a great weight would be lifted off her shoulders and found this promise very reassuring and very attractive. She also knew that if they turned this offer down, the family would lose their memories of this magical experience.

THE EPILOGUE

For the Jackson children, the magic had all started with the humming noise and orange light in the loft, followed by meeting a goblin. Then they met another goblin, followed by a ghost and later a huge mountain troll. After that they'd met three other goblins, an actual real-life dragon and finally the elven queen. The children had had one magical moment after another, transforming their reality from a normal life to a world of wonder and magic, and this had happened over a period of just four days.

Jenny on the other hand, had had her reality turned from normal to unbelievable, in one morning. Nevertheless, Jenny had listened to every word that Tinsel had said and by the afternoon, Jenny had agreed and the family had planned their return to the cave for the following weekend.

As well as their picnic, they would bring a supply of wood and firelighters, to build a fire in the cave entrance.

From that fire, a new dragon would be born.

AND SO IT BEGAN...

The Precious Dragon egg

Terry Brooks is quoted as saying:

'If you don't think there is magic in writing, you probably won't write anything magical.'

Lightning Source UK Ltd.
Milton Keynes UK
UKOW05f1247050617
302717UK00008B/100/P